ALSO BY ANNE RICE

Angel Time
Called Out of Darkness
Christ the Lord: The Road to Cana
Christ the Lord: Out of Egypt
Blood Canticle
Blackwood Farm
Blood and Gold
Merrick
Vittorio, The Vampire
The Vampire Armand
Pandora
Violin
Servant of the Bones
Memnoch the Devil
Taltos
Lasher
The Tale of the Body Thief
The Witching Hour
The Mummy
The Queen of the Damned
The Vampire Lestat
Cry to Heaven
The Feast of All Saints
Interview with the Vampire

Of Love and Evil

Of Love and Evil

THE SONGS OF THE SERAPHIM

A novel

Anne Rice

ALFRED A. KNOPF
New York • Toronto
2010

This Is a Borzoi Book
Published by Alfred A. Knopf
and Alfred A. Knopf Canada

Published in the United States by Alfred A. Knopf,
a division of Random House, Inc., New York, and
in Canada by Alfred A. Knopf Canada, a division of Random House of
Canada Limited, Toronto.
www.aaknopf.com   www.randomhouse.ca

Library of Congress Cataloging-in-Publication Data
Rice, Anne, [date]
Of love and evil : the songs of the seraphim, a novel / by Anne Rice. — 1st ed.
p. cm.
ISBN 978-1-4000-4354-5
1. Assassins—Fiction. 2. Angels—Fiction. 3. Rome (Italy)—Fiction. I. Title.
PS3568.I26504 2010
813'.54—dc22   2010028267

Library and Archives Canada Cataloguing in Publication
Rice, Anne
Of love and evil / Anne Rice.
(The songs of the seraphim ; 2)
Also available in electronic format.
ISBN 978-0-676-97809-4 (bound)
I. Title. II. Series: Rice, Anne. Songs of the seraphim ; 2.
PS3568.I22D93 2010   813'.54   C2010-901441-3

Manufactured in the United States of America
First Edition

For
my son,
Christopher Rice

and

For
my friend
Gary Swafford

Become my helper. Become my human instrument
to help me do what I must do on Earth.

Leave this empty life you've fashioned for yourself,
and pledge to me your wits, your courage, your cunning,
and your uncommon physical grace.

Say that you're willing, and your life is turned from evil,
you confirm it, and you're at once plunged into the
danger and heartache of trying to do
what is unquestionably good.

—The Angel Malchiah
speaking to Toby O'Dare in *Angel Time*

God appears, and God is light,
To those poor souls who dwell in night;
But does a human form display
To those who dwell in realms of day.

—From *Auguries of Innocence*
William Blake

We are, each of us angels with only one wing, and we can only fly by embracing one another.

—Luciano de Crescenzo

Of Love and Evil

CHAPTER ONE

I DREAMED A DREAM OF ANGELS. I SAW THEM AND I heard them in a great and endless galactic night. I saw the lights that were these angels, flying here and there, in streaks of irresistible brilliance, and some as great as comets which seemed to draw so close the fire might devour me, and yet I felt no heat. I felt no danger. I felt no self.

I felt love around me in this vast and seamless realm of sound and light. I felt intimately and completely known. I felt beloved and held and part of all I saw and heard. And yet I knew I deserved nothing of it, nothing. And something akin to sadness swept me up and mingled my very essence with the voices who sang, because the voices were singing of me.

I heard the voice of Malchiah rise high and brilliant and immense as he said that I must now belong to him, that I must now go with him. That he had chosen me as his companion and I must do what he would have me do. How strong and brilliant was his voice rising higher and higher. Yet there came against him a smaller voice, tender, lustrous, that sang of my life on Earth and what I had to do; it sang of those who needed me and loved me; it sang of common things and common dreams, and pitted these with faultless courage against the great things which Malchiah sought to do.

Oh, that such a mingling of themes could be so very magnificent and this music should surround and enfold me as if it were a palpable and loving thing. I lay upon the breast of this music, and I heard Malchiah triumph as he claimed me, as he declared that I was his very own. The other voice was fading but not conceding. The other voice would never concede. The other voice had its own beauty and it would go on singing forever as it was singing now.

Other voices rose; or they had been there all the while. Other voices sang all around me and of me, and these voices vied with angelic voices as though answering them across a fathomless vault. It was a weave, these voices, angelic and other, and I knew suddenly that these were voices of people praying, praying for me. They were people who had prayed before and would pray after and in the far future and would always pray, and all these voices had to do with what I might become, of what I might be. Oh, sad, small soul that I was, and how very grand was it, this burning world in which I found myself, a world that makes the very word itself meaningless as all boundaries and all measures disappear.

There came to me the blessed knowledge that every living soul was the subject of this celebration, of this infinite and ceaseless chorus, that every soul was loved as I was loved, known now as I was known.

How could it not be? How could I, with all my failures, all my bitter losses, be the only one? Oh, no, the universe was filled with souls woven into this triumphant and glorious song.

And all were known and loved as I was known and loved. All were known as even their prayers for me became part of their own glorious unfolding within this endless and golden weave.

"Don't send me away. Don't send me back. But if you must,

let me do your Will, let me do it with all my heart," I prayed, and I heard my own words become as fluid as the music that surrounded me and sustained me. I heard my own particular and certain voice. "I love You. I love You who made all things and gave us all things and for You I will do anything, I will do what it is You want of me. Malchiah, take me. Take me for Him. Let me do His will!"

Not a single word was lost in this great womb of love that surrounded me, this vast night that was as bright as day. For neither day nor night mattered here, and both were blended and all was perfect, and the prayers rising and rising, and overlapping, and the angels calling were all one firmament to which I completely surrendered, to which I completely belonged.

Something changed. Still I heard the plaintive voice of that angel pleading for me, reminding Malchiah of all that I was to do. And I heard Malchiah's gentle reproof and ultimate insistence, and I heard the prayers so thick and wondrous that it seemed I would never need a body again to live or love or think or feel.

Yet something changed. The scene shifted.

I saw the great rise of the Earth beneath me and I drifted downwards feeling a slow but certain and aching chill. *Let me stay,* I wanted to plead, but I didn't deserve to stay. It was not my time to stay, and I had to feel this inevitable separation. Yet what opened now before me wasn't the Earth of my expectations but vast fields of wheat blowing golden under a sky more vivid in the brightening sun than I had ever beheld. Everywhere I looked I saw the wildflowers, "the lilies of the field," and I saw their delicacy and their resilience as the force of the breeze bent them to and fro. This was the wealth of the Earth, the wealth of its blowing trees, the wealth of its gathering clouds.

"Dear God, never to be away from You, never to wrong You, never to fail You in faith or in heart," I whispered, "for this, all this You have given me, all this You have given us."

And there followed on my whisper an embrace so close, so total, that I wept with my whole soul.

The fields grew vague and large and a golden emptiness enveloped the world and I felt love embracing me, holding me, as if I were being cradled by it, and the flowers shifted and turned into masses of colors I couldn't describe. The very presence of colors we did not know struck me deep and rendered me helpless. *Dear God, that You love us so very much.*

Shapes were gone. Colors had detached themselves effortlessly from shapes, and the light itself was rolling now as if it were a soft and consuming smoke.

There appeared a corridor and I had the distinct impression, in words, that I had passed through it. And now, down the long corridor there came to me the tall slender figure of Malchiah, clothed as he always was, a graceful figure, like that of a young man.

I saw his soft dark hair, his oval face. I saw his simple dark suit with its narrow lines.

I saw his loving eyes, and then his slow and fluid smile. I saw him reach out to me with both arms.

"Beloved," he whispered. "I need you once again. I will need you countless times. I will need you till the end of time."

It seemed then the other voices sang from their hearts, in protest, in praise, I couldn't tell.

I wanted to hold him. I wanted to beg him to let me stay just a little while more with him here. Take me again into the realm of the lamps of Heaven. I wanted to cry. I had never known as a child how to cry. And now as an adult, I did it repeatedly, awake and in dreams.

7

Malchiah came on steadily as though the distance between us was far greater than I had supposed.

"You've only a couple of hours before they come," he said, "and you want to be ready."

I was awake.

The morning sun flooded the windows.

The noise of traffic rose from the streets.

I was in the Amistad Suite, in the Mission Inn, and I was sitting back against a nest of pillows, and Malchiah sat, collected and calm, in one of the wing chairs near the cold stone fireplace and he said again to me that Liona and my son would soon come.

CHAPTER TWO

A CAR WAS GOING TO PICK THEM UP FROM THE LOS Angeles airport and bring them straight to the Mission Inn. I'd told her I'd meet her under the campanario, that I'd have a suite for her and for Toby—that was my son's name—and that I'd take care of everything.

But I still didn't believe she'd really come. How could she come?

I'd disappeared out of her life, in New Orleans, ten years ago, leaving her seventeen and pregnant, and now I was back via a phone call from the West Coast, and when I'd found out she wasn't married, not even engaged, not even living with someone, when I'd found that out, I'd almost passed out on the spot.

Of course I couldn't tell her that an angel named Malchiah told me I had a son. I couldn't tell her what I'd been doing both before and after I met that angel, and I couldn't tell her when or how I might see her again.

I couldn't explain either that the angel was giving me time to see her now, before I went off on another assignment for him, and when she agreed to fly out here to see me, to bring my son, Toby, with her, well, I'd been in a sustained state of jubilation and disbelief.

"Look, the way my father feels about you," she'd said, "it's easier for me to fly to the West Coast. And of course I'll bring your son to see you. Don't you think he wants to know who his father is?"

She was still living with her father, apparently, old Dr. Carpenter, as I had called him back then, and it didn't surprise me that I had earned his contempt and scorn. I'd crept off with his daughter into the family guesthouse, and never dreamed all these years that she'd had a child as the result.

The point is: they were coming.

Malchiah went down with me to the front walk. It was perfectly plain to me that other people could see him, but he looked entirely normal, as he always did, a man of my height, and dressed in a three-piece suit pretty much like my own. Only his was gray silk. Mine was khaki. His shirt had a sheen to it, and mine was a workingman's blue shirt, starched, pressed and finished off with a dark blue tie.

He looked to me rather like a perfect human being, his wondering eyes drifting over the flowers and the high palms against the sky as if he was savoring everything. He even seemed to feel the breeze and to glory a little in it.

"You're an hour early," he said.

"I know. I can't sit still. I feel better if I just wait here."

He nodded as though that was perfectly reasonable when in fact it was ridiculous.

"She's going to ask what I've been doing all this time," I said. "What do I say to her?"

"You'll say only what's good for her and for your son," he answered. "You know that."

"Yes, I do," I conceded.

"Upstairs, on your computer," he said, "there's a long document you wrote called 'Angel Time.' "

"Yes, well, I wrote that when I was waiting for you to come

to me again. I wrote down everything that happened on my first assignment."

"That was good," he said, "a form of meditation and it worked well. But, Toby, no one must read that document, not now, and maybe not ever."

I should have known this. I felt a little crestfallen but I understood. With embarrassment I thought of how proud I'd been to recount my first mission for the angels. I'd even boasted to The Right Man, my old boss, that I had changed my life, that I was writing about it, that maybe someday he'd find my real name in the bookstores. As if he cared, the man who'd sent me as Lucky the Fox to kill over and over again. Ah, such pride, but then, in all my adult life, I'd never done anything before to be proud of. And The Right Man was the only person in this world with whom I had regular conversations. That is, until I had met Malchiah.

"Children of the Angels come and go as we do," Malchiah said, "only seen by a few, unseen and unheeded by others."

I nodded.

"Is that what I am now, a Child of the Angels?"

"Yes," he said, smiling. "That's what you are. Remember it."

With that he was gone.

And I was left realizing I had some fifty minutes to wait for Liona.

Maybe I'd take a little walk, have a soda in the bar, I didn't know. I only knew suddenly I was happy, and I was.

As I thought about this, I turned around, and looked towards the doors of the lobby, but for no particular reason. I saw a figure there, to one side of the doors, a figure of a young man, who stood with arms folded, leaning against the wall, staring at me. He was as vivid as anything around him, a tall man like Malchiah, only with reddish blond hair, and larger blue eyes, and he wore a khaki suit identical to my own. I turned my back on him to avoid his fixed stare, and then I realized how unlikely it was that the guy should be wearing a suit exactly like mine, and staring at me like that, with an expression that was just short of anger. No, it hadn't been anger.

I turned back. He was still staring. It was concern, not anger.

You're my guardian angel!

He gave me a near-imperceptible nod.

A remarkable sense of well-being came over me. My anxiety melted away. *I've heard your voice! I've heard you with the other angels.* I was fascinated and oddly comforted, and all of this in a split second.

A little crowd of guests came out of the lobby doors, passing in front of this figure, and obscuring him, and as they turned left to go along another path, I realized he had disappeared.

My heart was skipping. Had I seen all this correctly? Had he really been staring at me, and had he nodded to me?

My mental picture of this was fading rapidly. Someone had been standing there, yes, of course, but there was no way now to check what had happened, to submit it to any kind of analysis.

I put it out of my mind. If he was my guardian, what was he doing but guarding me? And if he wasn't, if he'd been someone else, well, what was that to me? My memory of this continued to fade. And of course, I'd settle the whole matter with Malchiah later. Malchiah would know who he was. Malchiah was with me. *Oh, we are creatures of such little faith.*

An extraordinary contentment filled me suddenly. You are a Child of the Angels, I thought, and the angels are bringing Liona and her son, your son, to you.

I took a long walk around the Mission Inn, thinking what a

perfect cool California day it was, passing all my favorite fountains and chapel doorways and patios and curios and other such things, and it was just time then for her to have come.

I returned to the far end of the walkway, near the doors to the lobby, and I waited for two likely people to start up the path and then pause under the low arched campanario with its many bells.

I couldn't have been there for longer than five minutes, pacing, looking around, checking my watch, moving in and out of the lobby now and then, when suddenly I realized that amid the steady flow of foot traffic along the path, there were two people standing right beneath the bells as I had asked those two people to do.

For a moment I thought my heart would stop.

I'd expected her to be pretty because she'd been pretty when she was a girl, but that had been the bud to this, the radiant flower, and I didn't want to do anything except stare at her, to drink in the woman she'd become.

She was only twenty-seven. Even I at twenty-eight knew that's not very old, but she had a womanly manner about her, and she was dressed in the most becoming and most finished way.

She wore a red suit, fitted at the waist and flaring over her narrow hips, with a short flared skirt that just covered her knees. Her pink blouse was open at her throat and there she wore a simple string of pearls. There was a tiny bit of pink handkerchief in her breast pocket, and her purse was patent leather pink, and so were her graceful high-heeled shoes.

What a picture she was in those clothes.

Her long full black hair was loose over her shoulders, with only some of it drawn back from her clear forehead and fixed perhaps with a barrette, the way she'd done it when she was a girl.

13

A sense came over me that I would remember her this way forever. It didn't matter what would happen next or hereafter. I would simply never forget the way she looked now, so gorgeous in red, with her full and girlish black hair.

In fact a passage came to me from a film, and it's one that many people love. It's from the film *Citizen Kane,* and an old man named Bernstein speaks the passage as he reflects on memory and how things can strike us that we see for no more than a few seconds. In his case, he's describing a young woman he once glimpsed on a passing ferryboat. "A white dress she had on," he says, "and she was carrying a white parasol. I only saw her for one second and she didn't see me at all, but I'll bet a month has not gone by since that I haven't thought of that girl."

Well, I knew that I would always remember Liona in that very way as to how she looked now. She was looking around, and she had about her the self-confidence and self-possession I remembered, and yet the pure uncomplicated courage that I had always associated with her simplest gestures or words.

I couldn't believe how lovely she was. I couldn't believe how simply, inevitably lovely she'd become.

But right beside her was the ten-year-old boy who was my son, and when I saw him, I saw my brother Jacob who'd died at that age, and I felt my throat tighten and the tears stand in my eyes. *This is my son.*

Well, I'm not going to meet them weeping, I thought, but just as I pulled out my handkerchief, she saw me and she smiled at me, and taking the little boy by the hand she brought him right up the path towards me, and she said in the most sprightly and confident voice,

"Toby, I would have known you anywhere. You look exactly the same."

Her smile was so vibrant and so generous that I couldn't

answer her. I couldn't speak. I couldn't tell her what it meant to me to see her, and when I looked down at the little boy looking up at me, this dark-haired, dark-eyed image of my long-dead brother Jacob, this perfect straight-shouldered and regal little boy, this confident and clever-looking little boy that any man would want for a son, this fine and splendid little boy, well, I did start to cry.

"You're going to make me cry if you don't stop," she said. She put her hand out and clasped my arm.

There was nothing hesitant or reticent about her, and when I thought back on it, I realized there never had been at all. She was forceful and confident and she had a deep, soft voice that underscored her generous character.

Generous, that was the word that came to me as I looked into her eyes, as she smiled up at me. She was generous. She was generous and loving and she'd come all the way here because I asked her to do it, and I found myself saying it out loud.

"You came. You came all the way. You came. I thought up until the last moment that you wouldn't come."

The little boy took something out of his breast pocket and he handed it to me.

I bent down the better to look at him, and I took what he had given me and I saw it was a little picture of me. It had been cut out of my school yearbook and it had been laminated.

"Thank you, Toby," I said.

"Oh, I always carry it," he said immediately. "I always tell people, 'That's my dad.' "

I kissed him on the forehead. And then he surprised me. He put his arm around me, almost as if he was the man and I was the boy. He put his arm around me and he held me. I kissed him again on his soft little cheek. He looked at me with the clearest simplest eyes. "I always knew you'd come," he said. "I mean I knew you'd show up someday. I knew you would." He said all that as simply as he'd said the rest.

I stood up, swallowed, and then I looked at both of them again, and put my arms around them both. I drew them close to me, and held them, and I was conscious of her softness, of her pure sweetness, a feminine sweetness so alien to me and the life I'd lived, and of a lovely floral perfume coming from her silky dark hair.

"Come on, the room's ready," I stammered as if these were momentous words. "I checked you in, let me take you up."

I realized then that the bellhop had been standing there all the while with the cart of luggage, and I gave him a twenty-dollar bill, told him it was the Innkeeper's Suite and we'd meet him on the top floor.

For a moment I merely looked at her again, and it came back to me what Malchiah had said. What you tell her, you tell her for her sake. Not for your own.

Something else hit me full force as I looked at her, as well, and that was how serious she was, that seriousness was the other side of her self-confidence. Seriousness was why she would pick up and come here without a moment's hesitation and let her son meet his father. And that seriousness reminded me of someone I'd known and loved on my adventures with Malchiah, and I realized now that when I'd been with that person—a woman in a long-ago age, I'd been reminded then of this beautiful and living and breathing woman who stood with me in my own day and age now.

This is someone to love. This is someone to love with all your heart the way you loved those people then, when you were with the angels, when you were with people you could never bring to your heart. All these ten years you've lived at a remove from every living being, but this is someone as real as Malchiah's people were real, a person that you can truly and totally love. Never mind whether or not you can get her to love you. You can love her. And this little boy, you can love him.

As we crowded into the little elevator together, Toby showed me other pictures of me from the yearbook. He'd been carrying them around for a long time too.

"So you always knew my name," I said to him, not knowing what to say really, and so stressing the obvious, and he replied that yes, he told everybody his daddy was Toby O'Dare.

"I'm glad. I'm glad you've done that. I can't tell you how proud I am of you," I said.

"Why?" he asked. "You don't even know what I'm really like." He was just small enough that his voice had a child's ring to it rather than an older boy's, and when he said these words they had a crisp clever sound. "I could be a bad student for all you know."

"Ah, but your mother was a brilliant student," I said.

"Yes, and she still is. She goes to Loyola to take courses. She's not happy teaching grammar school. She makes straight A's."

"And you do too, don't you?" I asked.

He nodded. "I'd skip a grade if they'd let me. They think it would be bad for my social development, and my grandfather thinks so too."

We'd come to the rooftop and I shepherded them around the balconies and then down the long red-tiled veranda. They had the suites in the hotel at the end of the veranda which were close to my own.

Now the Innkeeper's Suite at the Mission Inn is the only one that is really modern and lavish in the five-star sort of way. It's only available when the owners of the hotel aren't in residence, so I'd made certain that I could reserve it for this time.

They were suitably impressed with the three fireplaces, the immense marble bath, the lovely open veranda, and even more impressed when they discovered I'd engaged the adjacent room for Toby on the grounds that being ten years of age he might well want his own room and bed.

Then I took them into the Amistad Suite, my favorite, to show them the beautiful painted dome, and the tester bed, and the quaint fireplace that didn't work, and they did note it was very "like New Orleans" but I think they were thrilled with the luxurious digs they had, and so the whole thing went as I'd planned.

We sat down together at the iron-and-glass table, and I ordered some wine for Liona, and a Coke for Toby because he admitted that now and then, bad as it was for you, he did drink a Coke.

He took out his Apple iPhone and showed me all the things it could do. He had filed all the pictures of me in it and now, if it was all right with me, he was going to take a bunch more.

"Absolutely," I said, and he instantly became the professional photographer, backing up, holding the phone out the way an old painter might have held out his thumb, and photographed us from numerous angles as he moved around the table.

At this point, as Toby took picture after picture, a chilling realization descended on me. I'd done murder in the Amistad Suite. I'd done murder here at the Mission Inn, and yet I had brought these two people here as if this had never happened.

Of course Malchiah had come to me here, a Seraph who asked me why in the name of God I didn't repent of the miserable life I'd been living. And I had repented, and my entire existence had been forever altered.

He'd lifted me out of the twenty-first century, and sent me back in time to avert disaster for am imperiled community in medieval England. And when I'd finished that first assignment for my new angelic boss, I'd awakened here, at the Mission Inn, and it was here that I'd written out my entire account of that first journey into Angel Time. The manuscript was in the room. It was on the desk where I'd killed my last victim with a needle to the neck. And it was here that I'd called my old boss, The Right Man, and told him I would never kill for him again.

Notwithstanding, I'd done murder here. And it had been cold, calculated murder, the kind for which Lucky the Fox was justly famous. I shuddered inwardly, murmuring a prayer that no shadow of that evil would ever touch Liona or Toby, that no consequence of that evil would ever harm them.

This place had been my solace before that murder. It had been the one place where I felt at ease, and it was for this reason surely that I'd brought Liona and my son to this very spot, this very table where Malchiah and I had talked together. It seemed natural that they should be here, it seemed natural that I should experience this new joy of having them both, in this place where my grim, sarcastic prayers for redemption had actually been answered.

All right, my own ways made some sense to me. And what safer place was there for Lucky the Fox than the scene of his most recent crime? Who would ever expect a hired killer to go back to the scene of the crime? No one. I was confident of that. After all, I'd been a contract assassin for ten years and I'd never gone back to the scene of a single crime, until now.

But I had to admit, I'd brought these beloved innocents to a place of remarkable significance.

I was so unworthy of my long-ago love, and my newfound son, so utterly unworthy, and they had no conception of it.

And you had better make sure they never know, because if they do know who you were and what you did, if they ever glimpse the blood on your hands, you will have done them the most unspeakable harm and you know it.

I felt I heard a small voice, not very far away, say distinctly. "That's right. Not a word that could harm them."

I looked up to see a young man passing by, making his way along the wall, past the door of the Amistad Suite and off out of my vision. It was that same young man I'd seen below by the lobby doors, same suit identical to mine, and the shock of reddish blond hair, and the urgent engaging eyes.

I will not hurt them!

"Did you say something?" Liona asked.

"No, I'm so sorry," I whispered. "I mean I was talking to myself, I think. I'm sorry."

I stared at the door of the Amistad Suite. I wanted to get that murder out of my mind. The needle to the neck, the banker dying as if from a stroke, an execution carried out so smoothly no one had ever suspected foul play.

You are one coldhearted man, Toby O'Dare, I thought, that you could so easily seek to exploit a new lease on life at the very crossroads where you destroyed another's life with such abandon.

"I've lost you," Liona said gently with a smile.

"I'm sorry," I said. "Too many thoughts, too many memories." I looked at her and it was as if I were seeing her for the first time. Her face was so fresh, so trusting.

Before she could answer, we were interrupted.

One of the guides had come at my request, and I entrusted Toby to him for a tour of "the catacombs" and all the other wonders that the giant hotel had to offer. He was thrilled.

"We'll have lunch when you get back," I assured him. Though of course for them it would be an early supper as they had had lunch on the plane.

Now came the moment I had dreaded and most looked forward to, because Liona and I were alone. She'd taken off the red jacket, and she looked suitably shapely in the pink blouse and I felt an immense overwhelming desire to be with her, and to have nothing and no one interfere, and that included angels.

I was jealous of my son at that moment that he would very soon come back. And I was so aware of the angels watching that I think I blushed.

"How can you forgive me for disappearing like that?" I asked suddenly.

There were no tourists wandering the veranda. We were there alone at the glass table as I'd been so often in the past. We were sitting among the potted fruit trees and the lavender geraniums and she was the fairest flower of the lot.

"Nobody blamed you for going off," she said. "Everybody knew what had happened."

"They did? How?"

"When you didn't show up for graduation, they figured you'd been out playing for tips. And it was easy enough to find out that you'd played all night. So you'd come home in the morning and you'd found them there. And after that, well, you'd just left."

"Just left," I said. "I didn't even see to their burial."

"Your uncle Patrick took care of the whole thing. I think the fire department might have paid for it, or no, your father was a policeman. I mean I think that they paid. I'm not sure. I went to the funeral. All your cousins were out in force. People thought maybe you'd show up, but everybody understood when you didn't."

"I got on a plane for New York," I said. "I took my lute and the money I had and the few books I loved, and I got on a plane and I just never looked back."

"I don't blame you."

"But what about you, Liona? I never even called to find out how you were. I never even called to tell you where I'd gone or what I'd done."

"Toby, you know when a woman loses her mind like that, the way your mother did, when she kills her children—I mean when a woman does that, she can kill a boy your age too. There was a gun in the apartment. They found it. She could have shot you, Toby. She was just out of her mind. I didn't think about me, Toby. I just thought about you."

I didn't say anything for a long time. Then finally,

"I don't care anymore about it, Liona. What I care about is you forgive me that I never called you. I'll get some money to my uncle Patrick. I'll pay for the funeral. That's no problem. But what I care about is you. I care about you and Toby and I care about, well, the men in your life and what all that might mean."

"There are no men in my life, Toby," she said. "At least there weren't until you showed up. And don't think I expect you to marry Toby's mother. I brought Toby here for you and for him."

Marry Toby's mother. If I thought I could do that I would get down on my knees right here on this veranda and propose.

But I didn't do that. I was looking off and thinking of the ten years of my life I'd wasted, working for The Right Man. I was thinking of the lives I'd taken working for "the agency" or "The Good Guys" or whoever the hell it was to whom I'd so cheerfully and exuberantly sold my eighteen-year-old soul.

"Toby, you don't have to tell me what you've been doing," she said suddenly. "You don't have to explain to me what your life has been like. I haven't had a man in my life because I don't want my son to have a stepfather, and I was darned determined he was never going to have a stepfather of the month."

I nodded. I was more grateful for that than I could put into words.

"There haven't been any women for me, Liona," I said. "Oh, now and then, just to prove I was a man, I suppose, there was some contact. But that's all you'd call it: contact. Money was exchanged. It was never . . . intimate. It was never anything even approximating that."

"You've always been such a gentleman, Toby. You were that way when you were a boy. You use all the proper words for things."

"Well, it wasn't very often, Liona. And improper words would give it an exuberant color it never had."

She laughed. "Nobody talks like you do, Toby," she said. "I've never met anyone like you. Never anyone who even remotely made me think of you. I've missed *you.*"

I know I blushed. I was painfully aware of Malchiah and my guardian angel, whether they were visible or not.

And what about Liona's angel? Good Lord. For a split second I imagined a magisterial winged being behind her. Fortunately no such creature materialized.

"You still look innocent," she said. "You still have that same look in your eye—like everything you see is a miracle."

Me? Lucky the Fox, the contract killer? "You will never know," I murmured under my breath. I remembered that The Right Man had told me the night we met that I had the coldest eyes he'd ever seen.

"You're a bit heavier," she said, as though she'd just realized it. "More muscular, but I guess that's normal. You were so thin when you were a boy. But your head still has the same shape, and your hair's as thick as ever. I could swear you're more blond; maybe it's the California sun. And your eyes look almost blue sometimes." She looked away and said softly, "You're still my golden boy."

I smiled. I remembered now that she used to call me that, her golden boy. She would say that in a whisper.

I mumbled something softly under my breath about how I didn't know how to handle the compliments of beautiful women.

"Tell me about your studies," I said.

"English literature. I want to teach college. I want to teach Chaucer or Shakespeare, I haven't made up my mind which. I've had fun teaching grammar school, more fun than Toby cares to admit. He looks down on kids his age. He's like you are. He thinks he's a grown-up and he talks to grown-ups more than he does to children. It's his nature, just like yours."

We laughed at that because it was true. That's the nicest kind of soft laughing, when you laugh as an answer, or as punctuation, and southern people do that easily and all the time.

"Remember when we were kids we both wanted to be college teachers?" she asked. "Remember you said if you could teach college and own a beautiful house on Palmer Avenue, you'd be the happiest man in the world. Toby goes to school at Newman, by the way, and he'll tell you as soon as you ask him that it's the best school in town."

"It always was. Jesuit runs it a close second when it comes to high school."

"Well, some people would argue about who's on first when it comes to that. But the point is, Toby's Jewish and so he goes to Newman. My life's been happy, Toby. You didn't leave me in the lurch, you left me a treasure. And that's how I've always seen it, and that's how I see it now." She folded her arms and leaned forward on the table. Her tone was serious but matter-of-fact at the same time. "When I got on that plane, I thought, I'm going to show him this treasure that he left me. And I'm going to show him what that treasure might mean to him."

She stopped. I didn't say anything. I couldn't. And she knew it. She knew it by my tears. I couldn't put the fullness of happiness or love into words.

Malchiah, can I marry her? Am I free to do that? And what about that other angel, is he near me? Does he want me to reach across this table and take her in my arms?

CHAPTER THREE

WE DROVE OVER TO THE MISSION OF SAN JUAN CAPIS-trano that afternoon.

I figured there were many wonderful things for a little boy Toby's age to see on the West Coast, Disneyland, for one thing, and the park at Universal Studios, and other places of which I didn't know the names.

But the one place I wanted to take him was the mission and he seemed completely delighted by the idea, and though I had to provide watch caps for both of them, Liona and Toby both liked the Bentley convertible quite a lot.

When we reached the mission, I took them for a leisurely walk around the grounds, through the garden patches I loved, and around the koi pond, which delighted Toby. We looked at some of the mission exhibits that have to do with the way people did things in those days, but it was the story of the big earthquake that had destroyed the church which fascinated Toby the most.

He was having a lively time with his iPhone camera, and he took dozens of pictures of us in just about every setting imaginable.

Sometime or other, when we were browsing in the gift shop,

amid the rosaries and the Indian jewelry, I asked Liona if I could take Toby with me into the chapel and pray.

"I know he's Jewish," I said.

"It's fine," she answered. "You just take him and talk to him about it any way that you want."

We tiptoed inside because it was shadowy and quiet, and the few people at prayer in the plain wooden pews seemed very serious at it, and the candles gave a soft reverent glow.

I took him up to the front with me, and we knelt on the pair of prie-dieux that were there for weddings, for the bride and the groom.

I realized how much had happened to me with Malchiah since I'd come to this chapel, and when I looked at the tabernacle, when I looked at the small house of God on the altar, and the sanctuary light beside it, I was overcome with gratitude just for being alive, let alone being given a chance at life such as I'd been given, let alone being given the gift of Toby that was mine.

I leaned down close to him. He was kneeling there, with his hands folded just as mine had been folded, and he didn't seem to object to the fact that it was a Catholic house of worship.

"I want to tell you something, something I want you always to remember," I said.

He nodded.

"I believe God's in this house," I said. "But I know that He is everywhere too. He's in every molecule of everything that exists. It's all part of Him, His creation, and I believe in Him, in everything He's ever done."

He listened to this without looking at me. His eyes were down. He just nodded when I stopped.

"I don't expect you to believe in Him because I do," I said. "But I want you to know that I do believe in Him, and if I didn't think He'd forgiven me for leaving you and your mother, well, I don't know that I would have ever had the courage to pick up the phone and call her and tell her where I was. But I do believe He's forgiven me, and now it's my job to get you to forgive me, and to get her to forgive me, and I aim to do exactly that."

"I forgive you," he said in a small voice. "I really really do."

I smiled. I kissed the top of his head. "I know you do. I knew it when I first saw you. But forgiving doesn't really happen all at once, and sometimes it takes some maintenance, and I'm prepared for the maintenance that this is going to require. But . . . this isn't all I have to tell you. I have to tell you something else too."

"I'm listening," he said.

"Remember this," I said. I hesitated. I didn't know quite how to start. "Talk to God," I said. "No matter how you're feeling, no matter what you're facing, no matter what happens to hurt you or disappoint you or confuse you. Talk to God. And never stop talking to Him. You understand me? Talk to Him. Realize that because things go bad in this world, because they go well, because they come easy or they come with difficulty, well, it doesn't mean that He is not here. I don't mean here in this chapel. I mean here everywhere. Talk to Him. No matter how many years pass, no matter what happens, always talk to Him. Would you try to remember to do that?"

He nodded. "When do I start?"

I laughed softly under my breath. "Anytime you want. You start now with or without words, and you just keep talking and you never never let anything come between you and talking to God."

He thought about this very gravely and then he nodded. "I'm going to talk to Him now," he said. "You might want to wait outside."

I was amazed. I got up, kissed him again on the forehead and told him that I'd be right outside whenever he wanted to join me.

About fifteen minutes later he came out and we started walking down the garden paths together, and he was taking pictures again, and he didn't say too much. But he walked right close to me, next to me, as if he was with me, and when I saw Liona sitting on a bench just smiling at us as we walked together, I felt such happiness I couldn't find words myself to contain it. And I knew I never would.

We walked back, Toby and I, to the giant shell of the ruined church, the largest part that had been left by the old quake.

For the first time, I saw Malchiah, over to one side, leaning rather casually, for all his fine clothes, against the dusty brick-and-mortar wall.

"There he is again," said Toby.

"You mean you've seen him before?" I asked.

"Yeah, he's been watching us. He was in the chapel when we were in the chapel. I saw him when I was going out."

"Well, you could say I work for him," I said. "And he's keeping a bit of an eye on me."

"He's young to be somebody's boss," said Toby.

"Don't let him fool you," I said. "Hang here a minute. I think he wants a word with me and doesn't want to interrupt."

I crossed the broken ground until I caught up with Malchiah and I drew in close so that none of the tourists would hear what I had to say.

"I love her," I said. "Is that possible? For me to love her? I love him, yes, he's my son, and that's what I'm meant to do, and I thank Heaven for him, but what about her? Is there world enough and time to love her?"

"'World enough and time,'" he repeated smiling. "Oh, those are such beautiful words, and how you make me mindful of what it is I ask of you. World enough and time is what you have to give me," he said.

"But what about her?" I insisted.

"Only you know that answer, Toby," he said. "Or maybe I should say that the two of you know it. I think she knows it too."

I was about to ask about the other angel, but he left me.

How it looked to others I had no idea.

I found my son busy at the koi pond with his camera, determined to catch one fish which didn't want to be caught.

The afternoon went fast.

We shopped in San Juan Capistrano, and then I drove them along the coast. Neither of them had seen the Pacific and we found some breathtaking vantage points and Toby wanted to take as many pictures as he could.

Dinner was in the dark and atmospheric Duane's steak house, at the Mission Inn, and mother and son were suitably impressed. When nobody was looking Liona gave Toby a sip of her red wine.

We talked all about New Orleans the way it was these days after the horrors of Hurricane Katrina and how difficult the storm had been. I could tell it had been a great adventure to Toby, even though his grandfather made him do his homework in the motels they'd had to rent for the worst part of the aftermath, and that for Liona something of the old New Orleans was still gone.

"You think you'll ever come home to live there?" Toby asked.

"I don't know," I said. "I'm a creature of the coast now, I think, but there are different reasons why people live in different places."

And very quickly, heartbreakingly fast, he said, "I could live just fine out here."

There was a sudden flash of pain in Liona's face. She looked off, and then at me. I could scarcely disguise what I was feeling. Impulses, hopes, a sudden volcanic flow of dreams obliterated my thinking. There was a tragic quality to it. A grim pessimism took hold of me. *No right to her, no right to this.*

In the hazy gloom of the restaurant, I saw nothing. And then I realized I'd been looking at a pair of men at the table nearest us, Malchiah and my guardian angel. They sat still as a painting, regarding me just as figures in paintings often do, from the serene corners of their eyes.

I swallowed. I felt a rising desire. I didn't want them to know this.

At the door of her suite, she lingered. Toby had hurried off proudly to his *own* room, where he wanted to take his *own* shower.

Somewhere in the shadows of the veranda, those two were there. I knew it. I'd seen them when we came along the walkway. She didn't know. Maybe they weren't visible to her.

I stood silently, not daring to move closer to her, or to touch her arms, or to bend down for the smallest kiss. I was miserable with desire. I was in agony.

Is it possible for you two to understand this, that when I take this lady in my arms, she expects more from me than a brotherly embrace? Damn it, it's the gentlemanly thing to do, if only to give her the chance to say no to me!

Silence.

Maybe I could persuade you to go look out for somebody else for a while?

I distinctly heard the sound of laughter. It wasn't mean or derisive, but it was laughter.

I kissed her quickly, on her cheek, and went back towards my room. I knew she was disappointed. I was disappointed. Hell, I was furious. I turned around and leaned against the door of the Amistad Suite. Of course they were seated at the round table. Malchiah had the same serene and loving expression he always wore, but my guardian angel was anxious, if that was the right word, and he looked at me as if he were slightly afraid for me.

A torrent of angry words came to my lips, but the pair of them were gone just that quickly.

About 11:00 p.m., I got out of bed and went out on the veranda. I hadn't slept at all.

It was damp and cold, as it often was at night in California, even when the day has been mild. I deliberately let myself get miserably cold. I contemplated knocking on her door. I prayed. I worried. I watched. If I'd ever wanted anything more than I wanted her now, I couldn't remember it. I simply wanted her. Nothing in this world seemed more real than her body, inside that suite, lying in that bed.

I was suddenly ashamed. From the first moment I'd spoken to her on the phone, I'd imagined her in my arms and I knew it. Who was I kidding with all this, about her expecting things, and me being a gentleman, and, ah, the loftiness of love and being reunited and all of that. I wanted to kiss her and to have her. And why not, and was it right that I be tortured like this? Hell, I loved her. I had no doubt in my heart of hearts that I loved her. I could love her until the day I died. I didn't care what that meant, I was ready for it, all of it.

I was about to go back into my room, when I saw Malchiah standing nearby.

"Yes, what!" I demanded angrily.

This clearly startled him but he recovered immediately. I thought I saw a flicker of disappointment in his face. But he only smiled when he spoke. His voice was as always caressing, filled with a careful tenderness that made his words penetrate.

"Other humans would give almost anything to see the

proofs of Providence that you've seen," he said. "But you're still human."

"What would you know about that?" I asked. "And what makes you think I don't know all about it?"

"You don't mean what you say," he said soothingly. He sounded very convincing.

"You may have been watching humans since the dawn of time," I said, "but that doesn't mean you know what it's like to be one."

He didn't answer. His loving and patient expression made me furious.

"Are you going to be with me forever, till the day I give up the ghost?" I asked. "Will I never be alone again with a woman without you two being there, you and that guardian angel? That is what he is, right? My guardian angel? What's his name? Are you two going to be hovering over me forever?" I turned and jabbed my finger at him as if it were the barrel of a gun. "I'm a man," I said. "Human, a man! I'm not a monk, or a priest."

"You certainly lived like one when you were a killer."

"What do you mean by that?"

"You denied yourself the warmth and love of a woman year in and year out. You didn't think you deserved it. You couldn't bear to be around the innocence of women, or the warmth of a woman who might accept you. Do you deserve it now? Are you ready for it?"

"I don't know," I murmured.

"Do you want me to go away?" he asked.

I had broken out in a sweat, and my heart was racing.

"Simple desire is making a fool of me," I whispered. I think I was pleading with him. "No, I don't want you to go," I murmured. "I don't want you to." I shook my head, defeated.

"Toby, the angels have always been with you. They've

always seen everything that you've ever done. There are no secrets from Heaven. The only difference is, now you can see us. And that should be a source of strength for you. You know this. Your guardian angel's name is Shmarya."

"Look, I want to be filled with awe, with gratitude, humility, fine feelings! Hell, I want to be a saint!" I stammered. "But I can't be. I can't—. What did you say his name was?"

"Can't what?" he asked. "Can't live with restraint? Can't deny yourself the immediate gratification of your passions with this woman when you've been with her less than twenty-four hours? Can't keep yourself from running roughshod over her vulnerability? Can't be the honorable man your son might expect you to be?"

His words could not have stung more if they'd been spoken in anger. The gentle persuasive voice was fatal to all the lies I'd been telling myself.

"You think I don't understand," he said calmly. "I'll tell you what I think, that if you were to overwhelm that woman now, she would hate herself for it, and hate you too when she'd had time to think on it. For ten years, that woman has lived alone for the sake of herself and her son. Respect her. Win her trust. That takes times, does it not?"

"I want her to know that I love her."

"Did I say you couldn't tell her this? Did I say you couldn't have shown her some small measure of what you were holding in abeyance?"

"Oh, Angel Talk!" I said. I was furious again.

Once more, he laughed.

For a long moment we stood there in silence. I was ashamed again, ashamed of having gotten angry.

"I can't be with her now, can I?" I asked. "I'm not talking about desire. I'm talking about genuine love and companionship, and learning to love everything about her, being saved every day by her. You wanted me to know my son for his sake, and for her sake. But I can't have them both, not as an intimate part of my life, now, can I?"

"Yours has been a dark and dangerous path, Toby."

"Am I not forgiven?"

"Yes, you've been forgiven. But is it wise that you walk away from the kind of life you lived, without anticipating repercussions?"

"No. I think about that all the time."

"Is it right that you make no reparation?"

"No. I must make reparation."

"Is it right you break your vow to work with me to do good in this world, instead of evil?"

"No," I said. "I never want to break that vow, never. I owe the world a crushing debt for the things I did. Thank God, you've shown me a way to pay that debt."

"I will go on showing you," he said. "And in the meantime be strong for her, the mother of your son, be strong for him and the man he can become. And don't delude yourself as to the things you once did, the enormity of them. Remember that beautiful young woman has her angel, too. She doesn't begin to guess who you've been all these years. If she did, she might not let you near that child. Or so her angel reminds me."

I nodded. It was too painful to think about, too obvious to deny.

"Let me tell you something," he said. "Even if I left you now, if you never saw me again, if you came to believe that my visitations had been a dream, you could never slip into a settled domestic life without your conscience destroying you. Extraordinary deeds require extraordinary amends. Indeed, conscience can demand things of human beings that the Maker does not, and which angels do not suggest, because they have no need to do it. Conscience is part of being human. And your conscience was destroying you before I ever came to you. You've never been without conscience, Toby. Your guardian angel, Shmarya, could tell you that."

"I'm sorry," I said under my breath. "I'm sorry for all of this. I've failed you here. Malchiah, don't give up on me."

He laughed. It was a gentle reassuring laugh.

"You haven't failed me!" he said kindly. "Miracles happen in time for humans. And there isn't world enough and time for humans to get used to them. They never do. And I have been watching them since the dawn of time, yes. And humans are always surprising me."

I smiled. I was spent and far from serenity about any of it, but I knew he was speaking the utter truth, of course. The anger was gone.

"One thing more," he said warmly. His face was softened by an undeniable compassion. "Shmarya prompts me to say this," he confided, raising his eyebrows a little as he spoke. "He says if you cannot be a saint, or a monk or a priest, then think in terms of being a hero."

I laughed. "That's good," I said. "That's extremely good. Shmarya knows what buttons to press, doesn't he?" I laughed again. I couldn't help it. "When I feel like it, can I talk to him?"

"You've been talking to him for years," Malchiah said. "And now he's talking to you. And who am I to stand in the way of a beautiful conversation?"

I was alone on the veranda.

Just like that. Alone.

The night was empty. I was in my bare feet and they were freezing.

The next morning, I went to their suite to have breakfast.

Toby was up and dressed, in his blue blazer and khaki pants, and announced to me that he had slept in his own room and in his own bed.

I nodded as if that was what the world expected of young men of ten years of age, even if their mothers had giant king-sized beds in lavish hotel suites.

And we all had room service together at a beautifully draped table replete with hotel silver and the appropriate covers to keep the dishes deliciously hot.

I felt I couldn't take this parting.

I felt I just couldn't do it, but I knew full well it was what I had to do.

I'd brought my leather bag with me, and after the breakfast things were cleared away, I took out two folders from it and I put them in her hands.

"What is this?" she asked, naturally, and when I tried to explain that she could read all the material on the plane, she insisted I explain now.

"Trust funds, among other things, one for you, one for him, and an annuity that will pay monthly, a sum that's no problem for me, and ought to take care of all your expenses and his. And there's more where that came from."

"I haven't asked you for anything," she reminded me simply.

"You don't have to ask me. It's what I want for you both to have. There's enough there for him to go away to school, if you want him to. He could go to England, to Switzerland, to wherever the best education can be gotten. He could go for the summer, perhaps, and spend his regular years at home. I don't know about those things. I never did. But you know. And the people at Newman School know. And your father will know too."

She sat holding these folders, not opening them, and then tears began to slide down her cheeks.

I kissed her. I held her as tenderly as I could.

"Everything I have is now set aside for you and him," I said. "I'll send you more information when I have it. There are always so many questions lawyers ask and it takes such time."

I hesitated, then: "Look, a lot of things will puzzle you. My name doesn't appear in these papers, but be assured the name that does is one I use for business all the time. It's Justin Booth. I used it to pay for your airline tickets, and for the rooms at this hotel. And tell your lawyers the gift tax has been paid in full on everything being transferred to you and Little Toby."

"Toby, I never expected this," she said.

"Here's something else. This is a prepaid cell phone. Keep it close to you. The 'name' and pin number are on the back. That's all you need to renew the service. You can pay for it at any number of public places, simple as that. I'll call you on that cell."

She nodded gravely. There was something profoundly courteous in her accepting of these things, in not questioning why the secrecy, why the alias.

Again I kissed her, kissed her eyelids and her cheeks and then her lips. She was as tender and yielding as she'd ever been. The fragrance of her hair was the same as it had been so many years ago. I wanted to pick her up, carry her into the bedroom, take her, and bind her to me forever.

It was late. The car was already waiting downstairs. Little Toby had just come in to say that he was packed and ready for the plane. I don't think he liked my kissing his mother. He took a stand beside her, looking at me resolutely. And when I kissed him, too, he asked suspiciously, "When will we visit you again?"

"As soon as I can arrange it," I said. God only knows when that will be.

The walk downstairs was the longest walk I'd ever taken,

though Toby was delighted to be running up and down five flights of stairs in the rotunda, and listening to his voice echo off the walls.

He lost yet a little bit of his gentleman's polish at those moments.

All too soon, we were outside in front of the hotel, and the car was there.

It was another cool crisp blue California day, and all the flowers of the inn seemed to be at their most beautiful, and the birds were singing softly in the trees.

"I'll call you as soon as I can call you," I told her.

"Do something for me," she said under her breath.

"Anything."

"Don't tell me you'll call, if you won't."

"No, darling," I said. "I'll call you. I'll call you come Hell or high water. I just don't know when exactly that it will be." I thought for a moment, and then I said, "Give me world enough and time. Remember those words. If I'm late say them. Give me world enough and time."

I wrapped my arms around her and this time I kissed her, and I didn't care who saw us, even if it was Little Toby, and when I let her go, she took a step backwards as if she was as off balance as I was myself.

I picked him up and held him up and looked at him and then I kissed him on the forehead and on both cheeks.

"I knew you'd be like this," he said.

"If I'd told God Himself that I wanted a perfect son," I said, "and I'd had the nerve to tell God just how to make him, well, God couldn't have done any better, as far as I'm concerned."

Then the car was gone and they were gone, and the great beautiful world of the Mission Inn seemed empty as it had never seemed before.

CHAPTER FOUR

I'D REACHED MY SUITE BEFORE I DISCOVERED MALCHIAH waiting for me. He was seated at the black iron table and he was crying. He had his elbows on the table and his hands over his face.

"What's wrong with you!" I demanded. "What's the matter?" I sat down. "Is this my fault? What did I do?"

He sat back and slowly smiled the softest, saddest smile. "You really worried about me?" he asked.

"Well, yeah, you're crying. You looked heartbroken."

"I'm not heartbroken. But I think I could be. My fault for listening to the Schoolmen," he said. He meant the theologians of the universities, the men like Thomas Aquinas.

"You mean the men who say you have no heart."

"You made me cry, the three of you," he said.

"Why?"

He shrugged. "In your love for one another, I heard the echo of Heaven."

"Now you're bringing tears to my eyes," I said. I couldn't stop looking at him, at the depth of his expression. I wanted to put my arms around him.

"You needn't comfort me," he said with a smile. "But I'm moved that you want to do it. You can't know how mysterious it is to us, the way that humans love, yearning for completeness. Each angel is complete. Men and women on Earth are never complete, but when they reach for that completion in love, they reach for Heaven."

"Talk about mystery," I said. "You look like a man, you sound like a man, but you're not a man."

"No, I'm most certainly not."

"How do you look when you're before the Throne of God?" I asked.

He gave one of those soft reproving laughs. "I am a spirit before the Throne of the Maker," he said softly. "I'm a spirit now inhabiting a body made for this world. You know that."

"Are you ever lonely?"

"What do you think?" he asked. "Can I be lonely?"

"No," I said. "Hollywood movie angels are lonely."

"So true," he said smiling broadly. "Even I feel sorry for them. There'll come a time when you'll understand what I am because you will be like me, but I will never really know what it's like to be you now. I can only marvel at it."

"I don't want ever to be separated from them," I said. "My mind's working overtime on that. If I can't be with them, they'll hear my voice over the miles regularly and often. They're going to have anything that I can provide for them."

A sharp panic stopped me suddenly. The money I'd piled up all these years was blood money. But it was all I had, and I could use it for them, and it could be cleansed in that way, couldn't it? I couldn't take back the trust funds I'd already created. I prayed Malchiah would say nothing on this score.

"You belong to one another now," he said.

"What are you suggesting?" I asked. "Does that mean that someday somehow I might be with Liona and Toby under the same roof?"

He appeared to reflect for a moment, then he said:

"Consider what's already happened. By the love you now share, you're already transformed. Look at you. And in this brief visit you've altered the course of Liona's life and Toby's life forever. You'll never go a day of your life without knowing you have them, that they need you, that you mustn't disappoint them. And they will never experience a moment without knowing they have your love and acknowledgment. Don't you grasp the changes already taking place? Living under the same roof, that would be one aspect of this."

"That's a bloodless way of looking at it," I said, before I could check myself. "You don't know what it means for humans to live under the same roof."

"Yes, I do," he said.

I didn't answer.

He waited. I did see it, see how very enormous it was, what had happened with Liona and Little Toby, yet the concept of infinite possibilities spinning out from the moments we'd shared did not stop me from longing for so much more, I had to confess it.

"You know how to love," he said. "That is key. You can love not just those people you meet in the embracing illumination of Angel Time. You can love people in your own time. The woman and the boy didn't frighten you. Your heart beats with a new and practical love that two days ago was unimaginable to you."

I was too overwhelmed to reply. I pictured them again, Liona and Little Toby, as they'd looked when I first set eyes on them. "No. I didn't know I could love like that," I whispered.

"I know you didn't," he said.

"And I'll never disappoint them," I said. "But be merciful, Malchiah. Tell me I might one day live under the same roof with them. Tell me it's at least conceivable, whether I deserve it or not. Tell me I might somehow someday deserve it. Bear with me."

He was quiet for a moment. The tears were gone from his eyes. He looked placid and wondering. His eyes moved over me as though he were studying me. Then he looked at me directly.

"Perhaps," he said. "Perhaps there is world enough and time for that. Eventually. But you mustn't think on it now. Because now, it most likely cannot be." He paused as if he meant to say something else, and then thought the better of it.

"Can you make a mistake?" I asked. "I don't mean that I want you to, I only want to know. Can you be mistaken about something?"

"Yes," he replied. "Only the Maker knows all things."

"But you can't sin."

"No," he said simply. "Long ago, I chose for the Maker."

"Good God, can't you tell me—?"

"Not now, perhaps not ever," he said. "I'm not here to give you the history of the Maker and His angels, beautiful young man. I'm here to know you, and guide you, and ask of you that you give me your devoted service. Now leave your cosmic questions to Heaven, and let's get on with the work you must do."

"Oh, give me world enough and time to make up for the things I did, and world enough and time—."

"Yes, remember those words," he said, "where I'm sending you, because it will be a complex series of tasks. You don't go now to England, or that age, but rather to another in which things for the Jewish children of God are both better and worse."

"Then it's Jewish prayers we'll answer."

"Yes," he said, "and this time it is a young man named Vitale, and he is praying both desperately and faithfully for help, and you will go to him and find a complex of mysteries which only you can understand. But come. It's time we were on our errand."

WITHIN AN INSTANT WE HAD LEFT THE VERANDA behind.

I don't know what others saw if they saw anything.

I knew only we had left the solid world of the Mission Inn, and the solid world of Liona and Toby, and we were once again high in the clouds. If I had a form I couldn't see it or feel it. All I saw was the moist white swirling around me and here and there the tiniest flicker of a star.

I ached for the celestial music, but it did not come so much as the songs of the wind came, swift and refreshing and wiping me clean, it seemed, of all my thoughts of the recent past.

Suddenly below me I saw spread out an immense and seemingly endless city, a city of domes and rooftop gardens, and rising towers, and crosses beneath the ever shifting layers of clouds.

Malchiah was with me, but I couldn't see him any more than I could see myself. But I could see the familiar hills and tall pines of Italy, and I knew then that that was where I was going though to which city I was about to find out.

"This is Rome you see beneath you," said Malchiah. "Leo X sits on the papal throne, and Michelangelo, wearied from the accomplishment of his great chapel ceiling, labors on a dozen other commissions and will soon give himself to restoring St. Peter's itself. Raphael paints in glory the apartments that millions will come to see for centuries beyond this. But none of this is important to you, nor will I grant you even the smallest amount of time to glimpse the Pope or any of his retinue, for you are sent as always to one particular heart.

"This one young man, Vitale de Leone, prays urgently and faithfully, and so passionately do others pray for him that they are storming Heaven's gates."

Down we were moving, closer and closer to the rooftop gardens, closer to the domes and steeples, until finally we could see the maze of crooked stairways and alleyways that made up the streets of Rome.

"You yourself in this world are a Jew, named Toby, and you are a lutenist as you will soon discover, and let that be a key to you as to how much of your varied talent will be needed to see this venture through. Now you are known as one who is imperturbable and can bring consolation to the troubled through his music, so you will be welcomed when you arrive.

"Be brave, and be loving, and be open to all those who need you—especially to our frantic and much discouraged Vitale, who is a trusting man by nature, and who so valiantly prays for assistance. I count upon your cleverness as always, your nerve, and your cunning. But just as much I count upon your generous and educated heart."

CHAPTER FIVE

As I emerged onto a small piazza before a huge stone palazzo a crowd broke as if it had been waiting for me.

It was not the mob I'd encountered in England on my last escapade for Malchiah, but clearly there were goings-on here and I was being plunged into their very midst.

The crowd were Jews, almost all of them, or so it seemed because so many wore a round yellow circle attached to their clothes, and others wore blue tassels on the ends of their long velvet tunics. These were rich men, men of influence, and their bearing told me this as well as their dress.

As for me, I was dressed in a fine tunic of rolled velvet, with slashed sleeves with silver linings, leggings that were clearly costly and brightly dyed green and tall leather boots. I wore a pair of fine fur-trimmed leather gloves. On my back I carried by its thin leather strap a lute! I wore the round yellow patch as well. And when I realized this, I felt a certain vulnerability I'd never known before.

My hair was shoulder length and blond and curly, and I was more stunned by recognizing myself in this garb than by anything that the crowd before me might do.

They were one and all stepping aside for me and gesturing

to the gate of the house through which I could just see the light of the courtyard inside.

I knew this was my destination. No doubt of it. But before I could reach for a bell rope, or call out a name, one of the elders of the crowd stepped up as if to bar my way.

"You enter that house at your own peril," he said. "It's in the possession of a dybbuk. We have called the elders together three times to exorcise this demon, but we have failed.

"Yet the headstrong young man who owns the house won't leave. And now the world, which once trusted him and respected him, has begun to regard him with fear and contempt."

"Nevertheless," I said, "I'm here to see him."

"This is not good for any of us," said another one of the men present. "And your playing a lute for his patient is not going to change what is happening under this roof."

"What then would you say I should do?" I asked.

An uneasy laughter went through the group. "Stay clear of this house and stay clear of Vitale ben Leone until he determines to leave it and the owner decides to have it pulled down."

The house looked immense with four stories of round arched windows, and the action described seemed desperate.

"I tell you something evil has taken up its habitation here," said one of the other men. "Can you hear it? Can you hear the noises inside?"

I could in fact hear the noises inside. It sounded as if things were being thrown about. And it seemed that something made of glass was shattered.

I banged on the gate. Then I saw the rope for the bell and pulled hard on it. If the bell rang, it was deep within the interior of the house.

The men around me backed away as the gate finally opened,

and a young gentleman, about my age, stood squarely on the threshold. He had thick black shoulder-length curly hair and deep-set dark eyes. He was as finely dressed as I was in a padded tunic and leggings and he wore Moroccan leather slippers on his feet.

"Ah, good, you've come," he said to me, and without so much as a word to the others, he pulled me inside the courtyard of the house.

"Vitale, leave this place before you're ruined," said one of the men to him.

"I refuse to run," Vitale answered. "I will not be driven out. And besides, Signore Antonio owns this house and he is my patron and I do as he says. Niccolò is his son, is he not?"

The gate was shut and the heavy wooden door closed and bolted.

An old servant stood there holding a candle which he shielded with his skeletal fingers.

But the sharp light came from the high roof into the courtyard, and only when we started up the broad stone steps did we find ourselves plunged into shadow and in need of the little flame to guide our way.

It was like many an Italian house, showing only drab windowed walls to the streets, but its interior was worthy of the word "palazzo," and I was enthralled by the sheer size and solidity of it as we made our way through vast and polished rooms. I glimsed beautifully frescoed walls, floors of rich marble tile, and a wealth of dark tapestries.

A loud crashing noise sounded somewhere and this brought our little party to a halt.

The old servant uttered some prayers in Latin, and crossed himself, which surprised me, but the young man with me appeared fearless and defiant.

"I won't be driven out by it," he said. "I will find out what it is that it wants. And as for Niccolò, I will find a way to cure him. I am not cursed and I am no poisoner."

"That's what they're accusing you of? Of poisoning your patient?"

"It's because of the ghost. If it weren't for the ghost, I would be under no suspicion whatsoever. And because of the ghost I can't attend to Niccolò, which is what I should be doing now. I put the word out for you to play the lute for Niccolò."

"Then let's go to him, and I'll play the lute just as you've asked me."

He stared at me, indecisive, and then rattled again by a fierce crash that came from what might have been the cellar.

"Do you believe this is a dybbuk here?" he asked.

"I don't know."

"Come into my study." he said. "Let's talk just for a few minutes together before we go to Niccolò."

There were sounds now coming from everywhere, creaking doorways, and the sound of someone on a lower floor stomping his feet.

At last we opened the double doors of the study, and the servant quickly lighted several more candles for us as the shutters were drawn. The place was stacked with books and papers, and I could see glass cabinets of peeling leather volumes. It was plain some of these books were printed, and some were not. On the various small tables there were handwritten codices open, and on others papers filled with what looked like scribbling, and in the center of the room was the man's desk.

He gestured for me to take the Roman chair beside it. And then he flopped down, put his elbows on the desk and buried his face in his hands.

"I didn't think you would come," he said. "I didn't know who in Rome would play a lute for my patient now that I am in such disgrace. Only the father of my patient, my good friend Signore Antonio, believes that any measure I take might be helpful."

"I'll do whatever it is you need for me to do," I said. "I wonder if a lute might calm this troublesome spirit."

"Oh, what an interesting thought," he conceded, "but in this day and age of the Holy Inquisition, do you think one of us can dare to try to charm a demon? We'd be branded witches or sorcerers if we did this. Besides I need you badly at the bedside of my patient."

"Think of me as the answer to your prayers. I'll play for your patient and do whatever it is I can possibly do to help you with this spirit, also."

He looked at me for a long thoughtful moment, and then he said, "I can trust you. I know that I can."

"Good. Let me be of service to you."

"First listen to my story. It's brief and we have to be on our way, but let me tell you how it unfolded."

"Yes, tell me everything."

"Signore Antonio brought me here from Padua, along with his son Niccolò, who has become the closest friend I've ever had in the world, though I'm a Jew and these men are Gentiles. I was trained as a physician at Montpellier and that's where I first met father and son, and immediately began copying medical texts from Hebrew into Latin for Signore Antonio, who has a library five times the size of this which means everything to him. Niccolò and I were drinking companions as well as fellow students, and we went on, all of us, to Padua together and then finally home to Rome, where Signore Antonio set me up in this house to prepare it for Niccolò. It's for Niccolò and his bride, this house, but then the ghost appeared the very first night I knelt down and said my prayers here."

There came another loud crash from above and the distinct

sound of someone walking, though it seemed to me, in a house like this, one could not have heard the sound of an ordinary person walking.

The servant was still with us, crouched by the door, holding his candle. His head was bald and pink in the light with only a few wisps of dark hair, and he stared uneasily at the pair of us.

"Go on, Pico, get out of here," said Vitale. "Run to Signore Antonio and tell him I'm coming directly." Gratefully the man ran out. Vitale looked at me. "I'd offer you food and drink, but there's nothing here. The servants have run away. Everyone but Pico has run away. Pico would die for me. Perhaps he thinks that's what's about to happen."

"The ghost," I reminded him. "You said that he came the night you prayed. This meant something to you."

He fixed me seriously for a moment. "You know, I feel I've known you all my life," he said. "I feel I can tell you my most spiritual secrets."

"You can," I said. "But if we should see Niccolò soon, you'll have to speak quickly."

He sat still gazing at me, and his dark eyes had a low fire in them that I found rather fascinating. His face was filled with animation, as if he couldn't disguise any emotion, even if he wanted to, and he seemed at any moment about to burst into some wild exclamation but instead he grew quiet and began to talk in a low running voice.

"The ghost was always here, that's my fear. He was here and he will be here after we're forced out. The house has been shut up for twenty years. Signore Antonio told me that long ago he had let it to one of his earlier Hebrew scholars. He will say nothing else about the man except that he once lived here. Now, he wants the house for Niccolò and Niccolò's bride, and I'm to stay on, to be Niccolò's secretary, and physician when needed, and possibly the tutor to his sons when they're born. It was all such a happy scheme, this."

"And Niccolò was not ill yet."

"Oh, no, far from it. Niccolò was fine. Niccolò was looking forward to his wedding to Leticia. Niccolò and Lodovico his brother were making all kinds of plans. No, nothing bad had happened to Niccolò."

"And then you prayed that first night and the ghost began to trouble you."

"Yes. You see, I found the room upstairs which had been the synagogue. I found the Ark and in it the old scrolls of the Torah. These had belonged to that scholar whom long ago Antonio had let live here. I knelt down and I prayed, and I fear I prayed for things I had no right to pray for."

"Tell me."

"I prayed for fame," he said in a small voice. "I prayed for riches. I prayed for recognition. I prayed that, somehow, I'd become a great physician in Rome, and that I would be an outstanding scholar for Signore Antonio, perhaps translating texts for him that no one had yet discovered or made available."

"That sounds like a very human prayer to me," I said, "and given your gifts, it sounds quite understandable."

He looked at me so gratefully that it was heartbreaking. "You see, I have many gifts," he said humbly. "I have a gift for writing and reading that could keep me busy all my days. But then I have a gift as a physician as well, an ability to touch a man's hand and know what is wrong with him."

"Was it wrong then to pray that these gifts would flower?"

He smiled and shook his head. "You may have come to play the lute for my friend," he said, "but right now you give me more comfort than music ever could. The point is, that very night the ghost began his rumblings, his stampings, his casting things to the floor. It was right after my prayer, and always after he'd torn this study to pieces, and believe me, he can make the inkwells fly, he would retreat to the cellar. He would retreat and bang his fists against the casks of the cellar."

"My friend, this ghost may have had nothing to do with your prayer. Now go on. What happened with Niccolò?"

"Well, at this time Niccolò suffered a fall from a horse. It was nothing of any consequence and the wound healed instantly. Niccolò is stronger than I am. But ever since, he's been failing. He's grown pale. He shudders and I tell you every day he's worse and it's eating at his mind, this illness, this idleness, this lying in bed and watching his own hands tremble."

"The wound's clean? You're sure of it?"

"Certain. He has no fever from the wound. He has no fever at all. And the rumors, the rumors are spreading now as they always do, that I, his Jewish physician, am poisoning him! Oh, thank Heaven that Signore Antonio believes in me."

"This is a terrible danger, this being accused of poisoning," I said. I knew this well enough from history. No one had to tell me.

"Oh, understand, I have my indemnity from Signore Antonio, all properly signed, to treat the patient and that I'll be paid whether he lives or dies, and no accusation can formally be brought against me. That's the usual thing in Rome, and I have my dispensation from the Pope to treat Christians. I've had that for years. I'm dispensed from wearing the yellow patch. All that's in order. My concern is not what will become of me. My concern is this ghost and why he's here. And my concern is what will happen to Niccolò. I love Niccolò! If it weren't for the ghost I wouldn't be accused. And my other patients wouldn't have fled. But I could do without them. I could do without it all. If only Niccolò were well. If only Niccolò were restored. But I must discover why this ghost plagues me and why I cannot cure Niccolò there where he lies not one hundred feet from here in his own house growing ever weaker."

"We should go to Niccolò. We can talk of the ghost later."

"Oh, but one thing first. I prayed with pride that first night. I know that I did."

"We all do, my friend. It's pride, is it not, to ask God for anything? And yet He tells us to ask. He tells us to ask as Solomon asked for wisdom."

He drew back and that seemed to calm him. "As Solomon asked," he whispered. "Yes. I did that. I told him I wanted to have all these many gifts, gifts of the spirit and the mind and the heart. But did I have the right to do it?"

"Come now," I said. "Let's go to your friend Niccolò."

He paused as though listening for some distant sound. And we both realized the house was quiet, and had been for some time.

"Do you imagine the dybbuk has been listening?" he asked.

"Perhaps," I said. "If he can make a sound, then he can hear a sound, isn't that likely?"

"Oh, may the Lord bless you, I am so glad you came to me," he said. "Let's be going."

He clutched my hand with both of his. He was a passionate man, a volatile man, and I realized how very different in spirit he was from those I'd visited on my last adventure, who for all their passion had not had his hot southern Mediterranean blood.

"You realize I don't know your name?" he asked.

"Toby," I said. "Now let's go to see your patient. While I play the lute, I can listen and I can watch and I can see if in fact this man is being poisoned."

"Oh, but that's not possible."

"I don't mean by you, Vitale, I mean by someone else."

"But I tell you, Toby, there is no one that does not love him, no one that could bear to lose him. Therein lies the dreadful mystery."

We found the same crowd in the street, but this time the Jews had been joined by some onlookers and some of the rougher sort and I didn't like the look of it.

We pushed through without speaking a word, and as we made our way through the thick press of the alleyway, Vitale was whispering to me.

"Things are good here now for the Jews," he said. "The Pope has a Jewish physician and he's my friend, and there are Jewish scholars in demand everywhere. I think that every cardinal must have a Hebrew scholar on his staff. But that could change in an instant. If Niccolò dies, the Lord have mercy on me. With this dybbuk I will be accused not only of poison but of witchcraft."

I nodded to this, but was mainly trying to make my way through the press of passersby, peddlers and beggars. The cookshops and taverns added their scents and swell to the narrow street.

But within minutes, we had arrived at the house of Signore Antonio, and were admitted at once through its huge iron gates.

CHAPTER SIX

IMMEDIATELY WE ENTERED A HUGE COURTYARD, FILLED with potted trees, arranged at random around a glittering fountain.

The bent and withered old man who opened the gate for us was shaking his head and very forlorn.

"He's worse today, young Master," he said, "and I fear for him, and his father has come downstairs, and will not leave the bedside. He waits for you now."

"That's good, Master Antonio is out of bed, that's very good," said Vitale immediately. He confided to me, "When Niccolò suffers, Antonio suffers. The man lives for his sons. He has his books, his papers, his work for me all the time, but without his sons, there's nothing really for him."

Together we went up a very broad and impressive stairway of shallow treads and polished stone. And then proceeded down a long gallery. There were spectacular wall hangings everywhere, tapestries of wandering princesses and gallant young men at the hunt, and great sections of the wall painted in brilliant pastoral frescoes. The work looked as fine to me as if it had been done by Michelangelo or Raphael, and for all I knew some of it had been done by their apprentices or students.

We passed now into a chain of antechambers, all with marble tiled floors and scatterings of Persian and Turkish carpets. Magnificent classical scenes of nymphs dancing in paradisal gardens adorned the bare walls. Only an occasional long table of polished wood stood in the center of a room. There were no other furnishings.

Finally the double doors were thrown open to a vast and ornate bedroom, darkened, except for the light that came in with us, and there lay Niccolò, obviously, pale and bright-eyed against a mound of linen pillows beneath a huge red-and-gold baldachin.

His hair was blond and full and matted to his damp forehead. In fact, he looked so feverish and so restless that I wanted to demand someone bathe his face immediately.

It was also plain to me that he was being poisoned. I could tell that his vision was blurred and his hands were trembling. For a moment he stared at us as if he couldn't see us.

I had the sinking feeling that the poison had already reached the fatal level in his blood. I felt a slight panic.

Had Malchiah sent me here to know the bitterness of failure?

Beside the bed sat a venerable gentleman in a long burgundy velvet robe, with black stockings and slippers of jeweled leather. He had a full head of near-lustrous white hair, with a widow's peak that gave him considerable distinction, and he brightened at the sight of Vitale. But he didn't speak.

On the far side of the bed stood a man who seemed so deeply moved by all this that his eyes were wet with tears and his hands were shaking almost as badly as the patient's hands were shaking.

I could see he bore some resemblance to the old man and to the young man in the bed, but something very different marked his appearance. He lacked the hairline for one thing, and he also had larger and much darker blue eyes than either of the others, and whereas the old man expressed his concern in a devout manner, this young man seemed in the midst of breaking down.

Beautifully dressed in a gold-trimmed tunic with slashed sleeves and silk lining, he wore a sword at his hip, and he was clean shaven with short curly black hair.

All this I took in almost immediately. Vitale kissed the ring of the gentleman seated by the bed, and he said in a low voice,

"Signore Antonio, I am glad to see you downstairs, though sad that you must see your son like this."

"Tell me, Vitale," asked the old man. "What is the matter with him? How could a simple injury falling from a horse produce a condition so miserable as this?"

"This is what I mean to discover, Signore," said Vitale. "I give you my heart as my pledge."

"You once cured me when every Italian physician had given me up for dead," said Signore Antonio. "I know that you can heal my son."

The young man on the far side of the bed became all the more agitated. "Father, though it pains me to say it, we had best listen to the other doctors. I am in terrible fear. My brother lying here is not my brother." The tears welled in his eyes.

"Yes, this diet of caviar I accept, Lodovico," said the patient to the young man. "But Father, I have complete trust in Vitale just as you trusted in Vitale, and if I'm not to be cured, then it's God's Will."

He narrowed his eyes as he looked at me. He was puzzled by me, and every word he spoke was an effort.

"A diet of caviar?" asked the father. "I don't understand."

"That my brother take caviar for the purity of it," said the young man, Lodovico, "and that he take it three times a day and no other food. I went to the Pope's physicians for their advice on this. I am only doing what they have told me to do. He has taken this diet now since the fall."

"Why was I not told this?" asked Vitale, glancing at me, as he spoke, then at Lodovico. "Caviar and nothing else? You are not satisfied with the food I recommended?"

I saw the anger flash in Lodovico's eyes for an instant, then fade at once. He was too distraught apparently to be insulted.

"My brother was not doing well on such food," he said with a half smile that quickly faded. "The Holy Father himself has sent the caviar," he went on patiently to explain to the father, expressing an almost tender trust. "His predecessor swore by it. And he lived well and was hearty and it gave him strength."

"No insult to His Holiness," said Vitale quickly, "and it's kind of him to send this caviar, of course. But I've never heard of anything so strange."

He glanced meaningfully at me, but I doubt anyone else saw it.

Niccolò tried to sit up on his elbows and then sat back, too weak, but still determined to speak.

"I don't mind it, Vitale. It has some taste to it and it seems I can taste nothing else." He sighed rather than spoke, and then he murmured, "It burns my eyes, however. But then probably any other food would do as much."

It burns my eyes.

My mind was mulling over this uneasily. No one had the slightest notion of course that I was a man who'd concocted poisons, disguised poisons and knew how to give them, and if ever there was a food that could mask a poison it was pure black caviar, because you could slip just about anything into it in this world.

"Vitale," the patient asked. "Who is this man who's come with you?" He looked up at me. "Why are you here?" It was a struggle for him to get these words out of his mouth.

And finally, much to my relief, a servant woman appeared with a basin of water, and applied a cold rag to his head. She wiped some of the sweat from his cheeks. He was annoyed by it and motioned for her to stop, but the old man directed her to go on.

"I've brought this man to play the lute for you," explained Vitale. "You know how music has always soothed you. He'll play softly, nothing that agitates you."

"Oh, yes," said Niccolò settling back on the pillow. "That is a kind thing indeed."

"The rumor is in the street that you hired this man to play for the demon in your house," said Lodovico suddenly. Again he looked to be on the verge of tears. "Is that what you did? And you lie about it now, you say this as a ruse?"

Vitale was shocked.

"Lodovico, stop," said the father. "There is no demon in that house. And never have I heard you speak to Vitale like this. This is the man who nursed me back to health when every doctor in Padua, where there are indeed more doctors than anywhere else in Italy, had given me up for dead."

"Oh, but Father, there is an evil spirit in that house," said Lodovico. "All the Jews know it. They have a name for it."

"Dybbuk," said Vitale wearily, and a bit fearlessly for a man who had a ghost in his house.

"This man's been plagued by this dybbuk since you gave him the keys," Lodovico went on. "And it was only after this dybbuk took up residence and started breaking windows in the dead of night that Vitale's skills as a physician have disintegrated before our very eyes."

"Disintegrated?" Vitale was stunned. "Who says my skills are disintegrated? Lodovico, this is a lie!" He was hurt, confused.

"But the Jewish patients won't come to you, will they?"

asked Lodovico. Suddenly, he changed his tone. "Vitale, my friend, for the love of my brother, tell the truth."

Vitale was stymied. But Niccolò only looked at him trustingly and lovingly, and the old man was thoughtful and not quick to say anything at all.

"The Jews have told us this themselves," said Lodovico. "Three times they've tried to drive this dybbuk from your house. This dybbuk is in your study, in the room where you keep your medicines, this dybbuk is in every corner of your house and in every corner perhaps of your mind!"

The young man was working himself into a frenzy.

"No, you must not say those things," said Niccolò in a loud voice. Vainly he tried again to raise himself on his elbows. "It's not his doing that I'm ill. Do you think every man who takes a fever and dies of it does so because there's a demon in a house in the same street? Stop saying such things."

"Quiet, my son, quiet," said the old man. He laid his hands on his son and tried to force him back against the pillow. "And remember, my sons, the house in question is mine. Therefore the demon, or the dybbuk as the Jews call it, must certainly belong to me. I must go to the house and confront this awesome spirit who routs exorcists both Jewish and Roman. I must see this spirit with my own eyes."

"Father, I beg you, don't do that!" said Lodovico. "Vitale isn't telling you of the violence of this spirit. Every Jewish doctor who's come here has told us. It hurls things and breaks things. It stomps its feet."

"Oh, nonsense," said the father. "I believe in illness and I believe in cures for it. But in spirits? Spirits who hurl things? This I'll have to see with my own eyes. It's enough for me that Vitale is here with Niccolò."

"Yes, Father," said Niccolò, "and this is enough for me.

Lodovico, you've always loved Vitale," he said to his brother, "the same as I have. The three of us, we've been friends since Montpellier. Father, don't listen to these things."

"I'm not listening, my son," said the father, but the father was now carefully observing his son, because the more the son protested, the sicker he looked.

Lodovico knelt down beside the bed and wept with his forehead on his arm. "Niccolò, I would do anything in my power to see you cured of this," he said, though it was difficult to understand him through his tears. "I love Vitale. I always have. But the other doctors, they say he's bewitched."

"Stop, Lodovico," said the father. "You alarm your brother. Vitale, look at my son. Examine him again. That's why you've come."

Vitale was watching all of this keenly, and so was I. I couldn't detect the poison by any scent in the room, but that meant nothing. I knew any number of poisons, which slipped into caviar would do the trick. One thing was clear, however. The patient still had considerable strength.

"Vitale, sit with me," said the patient. "Stay with me today. The worst thoughts have been coming to me. I see myself dead and buried."

"Don't say this, my son," said the father.

Lodovico was past all comfort.

"Brother, I don't know what life means without you," he said tenderly. "Don't make me contemplate it. The first thing I remember is your standing at the foot of my cradle. For me, as well as for Father, you must get well."

"All of you, leave us, please," said Vitale. "Signore, you trust me here as you always have. I want to examine the patient, and you, Toby, take a place there"—he pointed to the far corner—"and play softly to still Niccolò's nerves."

"Yes, that's good," said the father, and he rose and beckoned for the younger man to come out.

The younger man didn't want to do it.

"Look, he's scarce tasted the caviar last given to him," said Lodovico. He pointed to a small silver plate on the bedside table. The caviar sat in a tiny glass dish inside it with a small delicate silver spoon. Lodovico filled the spoon and brought it to Niccolò's lips.

"No, no more. I tell you, it burns my eyes."

"Oh, come, you need it," said the brother.

"No, no more, I can't bear anything now," said Niccolò. Then as if to quiet his brother, he took the spoon and swallowed the caviar and at once his eyes began to redden and tear.

Once again Vitale asked that all go out. He gestured for me to sit down in the corner, where a huge fantastically carved black chair glowered as if waiting to devour me.

"I want to remain here," said Lodovico. "You should ask me to remain here, Vitale. If you are accused—."

"Nonsense," said the father, and taking the son's hand he led him from the room.

I settled snugly into the huge chair, a veritable monster of exuberant black claws, with red cushions for the back and for the seat. I removed my gloves, slipping them behind my belt, and I began to tune the lute as softly as I could. And it was a beauty. But other thoughts were playing in my mind.

The patient hadn't been poisoned until the dybbuk had appeared. Surely the poisoner was here, in this house, and I was fairly certain it was the brother, who was taking advantage of the appearance of the ghost. I doubted the poisoner was clever enough to produce a ghost. In fact, I was sure that the poisoner had not produced the ghost. But he was clever enough to begin his evil work because a ghost had appeared.

I began to play one of the very oldest melodies that I knew, a little dance based on a few basic chord variations, and I made the music as gentle as I could.

The thought struck me, as was inevitable, that I was actually playing a fine lute in the very period in which it had become wildly popular. I was in the very age in which it had attained perhaps its greatest music and strength. But there was no time for indulging myself in this, any more than there was time for making for St. Peter's Basilica to see the construction for myself.

I was thinking about the poisoner and how fortunate we were that he had chosen to take his time.

As for the mystery of the dybbuk, it had to wait on the mystery of the poisoner because clearly the poisoner, though patient, did not need very much more time to accomplish what he'd set out to do.

I was strumming slowly when Vitale gently gestured for me to be quiet.

He was holding his patient's hand, listening to his pulse, and now very gracefully he bent down and put his ear to Niccolò's chest.

He placed both his hands on Niccolò's head and looked into his eyes. I could see Niccolò shuddering. The man couldn't control it.

"Vitale," he whispered, thinking perhaps I couldn't hear him. "I don't want to die."

"I won't let you die, my friend," said Vitale desperately. He laid back the bedclothes now and examined his patient's ankles and feet. True, there was an old discolored patch on the ankle but it was no cause for alarm. The patient could move his limbs well enough but they shuddered. That could mean any number of poisons attacking the nervous system. But which one, and how would I prove who was doing it and how?

I heard a sound in the passage. It was the sound of a man crying. I knew by the very sound of it that it was Lodovico.

I got up. "I'll talk to your brother, if I might," I said softly to Niccolò.

"Console him," said Niccolò. "Let him know that none of this is his doing. The caviar has helped me. He puts such store by it. Don't let him feel that he's at fault."

I found him stranded in the antechamber, looking lost and confused.

"May I talk with you?" I asked gently. "While he's resting, or being examined? May I be of some comfort to you?"

I felt the strong urge to do this, when in fact, in the usual course of things, it was something I wouldn't have done at all.

However, he looked to me at that moment like one of the loneliest beings I'd ever beheld. He seemed to exist in a pure isolation as he wept, staring at the door of his brother's room.

"He is the reason my father has accepted me," he said under his breath. "Why do I tell you this? Because I must tell someone. I must tell someone how troubled I am."

"Come, is there someplace where we might talk in quiet? It is so difficult when those we love are suffering."

I followed him down the broad stairway of the palazzo and into the large courtyard, and into yet another gated courtyard which was wholly unlike the first, in that it was crowded with tropical blooms.

I felt the hair rise on the back of my neck.

A good deal of light spilled down into the area though the palazzo must have been four stories high, and the area was naturally sheltered due to its smaller size. It was extremely warm.

I could see orange trees and lemon trees, and purple flowers and waxen white blooms. Some of these I knew and some I didn't. But if there were no poisonous plants in this room, then my mother had raised a fool.

In the center of the courtyard, where the shafts of sunlight made a sweet and beautiful light, stood a makeshift cross-legged writing table and two simple chairs beside it. There was a decanter of wine and two goblets.

And the dejected man, moving almost as if in a dream, took the decanter, filled a goblet and drank the contents down.

Only then did he think to offer me a drink, and I declined.

He seemed exhausted and emptied from his weeping. That he was genuinely miserable was beyond doubt. Indeed he was grieving, and I wondered if he was grieving because in his mind and heart his brother was already dead.

"Sit down there, please," he said to me, and then he collapsed at his writing table, allowing a whole sheaf of papers to fall to the floor.

Behind him, from a large pot, grew a rangy and waxen-leafed tree, and one that was not at all unfamiliar to me. Again the hair rose on the back of my neck and my arms. I knew the purple flowers that covered this tree. And I knew the tiny black seeds that were left when the flowers dropped, as some of them had already done into the moist earth of the pot.

I picked up the mess of papers and put them back on the desk. I set my lute beside the chair.

The man appeared dazed as he watched this, and then he leant on his elbows and he wept very genuine tears.

"I have no great gift for poetry, and yet I am a poet for want of being anything else," he said to me. "I've traveled the world, and have had the joy of it—no, maybe all the joy of it was writing to Niccolò and meeting him if and when he'd come to me. And now I have to think of the vast wide world, the world I traveled, without him. And when I think of this, there is no world."

I stared past him at the earth in the pot. It was covered with black seeds. Any one of these would have been deadly to a child. Several, carefully chopped, would be deadly to a man. A small portion given regularly in caviar, of all perfect things, would have sickened the man slowly and pushed him closer with every dose towards death.

The taste of the seeds was ghastly, as is the case with many a poison. But if anything would hide it, it would be caviar.

"I don't know why I tell you these things," said Lodovico, "except that you look kind, you look like a man who peers inside another man's soul." He sighed. "You grasp how a man might love his brother unbearably. How a man might think himself a coward when faced with his brother's weakness and death."

"I want to understand," I said. "How many sons does your father have?"

"We are his only sons, and don't you know how much he will despise me if Niccolò is gone? Oh, he loves me now, but how he will despise me if I am the survivor. It was only on account of Niccolò that he brought me from my mother's house. We don't have to talk of my mother. I never talk of her. You can well understand. My father need have acknowledged no claim against him. But Niccolò loved me, loved me from the first moment we played as children, and one day, I, and all I possessed, were bundled up and taken from the brothel in which we lived, and brought here, to this very house. My mother took a fistful of gems and gold for me. She cried. I will say that much for her. She wept. 'But this is for you,' she said. 'You, my little prince, are now to be taken to the castle of your dreams.' "

"Surely she meant it. And the old man. He seems to love you so, as much as your brother."

"Oh, yes, and there were times when he loved me more. Niccolò and Vitale, what rascals they can be when they get together. I tell you, there's not much difference between a Jew and a Gentile when it comes to wenching and drinking, at least not all of the time."

"You are the good boy, aren't you?" I asked.

"I've tried to be. With my father, I went on our travels. He couldn't pry loose Niccolò from the university. Oh, I could tell you stories of the wilds of America, the wilds of Portuguese ports and savages such as you can only imagine."

"But you came back to Padua."

"Oh, he would have me educated. And in time that meant the university for me as well as my brother, but I could never catch up with them in their studies, Vitale, Niccolò, any of them. They helped me. They always took me under their wing."

"So you had your father to yourself those years," I said.

"Yes," he said. The tears were frozen now, no longer slipping down his face. "Yes, and you should have seen how quickly he embraced my beloved brother. Why, you would think he had left me in the jungles of Brazil."

"That plant there, that tree," I said. "It's from the jungles of Brazil."

He stared fixedly at me, and then turned and appeared to stare at the plant as though he'd never seen it before. "Perhaps it is," he said. "I don't remember. We brought back many a sapling and many a cutting with us. Flowers, you see, he loves them in profusion. He loves the fruit trees that you see blooming here. He calls this his orangery. It's his garden, really. I only come here now and then to write my poems as you can see."

The tears were entirely gone.

"How would you know such a plant on seeing it?" he asked.

"Hmmm, I've seen it in other places," I ventured. "I've even seen it in Brazil."

His face had changed and now he seemed calculatedly to soften as he looked at me.

"I understand your worry for your brother," I said, "but perhaps he will recover. There's a great deal of strength in him yet."

"Yes, and then perhaps my father's plans for him may begin in earnest. Except there is a demon standing between him and those very plans."

"I don't follow you. Surely you don't think your brother . . ."

"Oh, no," he said coolly, his tears having dried. "Nothing of the sort." Then he looked dazed again and preoccupied, and he raised one eyebrow and smiled as if he were lost in his innermost thoughts.

"The demon stands in my father's way," he said, "in a manner you can't have known. Let me tell you a little story of my father."

"By all means do."

"Kindly he is, and all those years kept me at his side like his trained monkey, from ship to ship, his beloved little pet."

"Those were happy times?"

"Oh, very."

"But boys become men," I interjected.

"Yes, precisely, and men have desires, and men can feel a love so keen it's as if a dagger has pierced the heart."

"You have felt such a love?"

"Oh, yes, and for a perfect woman, a woman with no cause to look down on me, born as she was, the secret daughter of a rich priest. I needn't tell you his name for you to grasp the threads here. Only that when I set eyes on her, there was no world but the world in which she existed, there was no place where I would ever want to roam unless she were at my side." He looked at me again fixedly, and then that dazed expression overtook him. "Was it such a fantastic dream?"

"You love her, and you want her," I coaxed.

"Yes, and wealth I have from my father's ever-increasing

generosity and affection, abundantly in private, and in the presence of others."

"So it seems."

"Yet when I proposed to him her very name, what do you think the course of action suddenly became? Oh, I wonder that I hadn't seen it. I wonder that I hadn't understood. Daughter of a priest, yes, but such a priest, such a high-placed cardinal with so many rich daughters. How could I have been a fool not to see he saw her as a crowning jewel for his elder son."

He stopped. He looked at me intently.

"I don't know who you are," he said musing. "Why do I tell you of the ugliest defeat of my life?"

"Because I grasp it," I said. "He told you the woman was for Niccolò, not for you."

His face became hard and almost vicious. Every line in it that a moment ago had seemed pregnant with sorrow and concern now hardened into a mask of coldness that was frightening, and would have been to anyone who saw him as he was.

He raised his eyebrows and gazed past me coldly.

"Yes, for Niccolò, my beloved Leticia was intended. Why hadn't I known that the talks had already begun? Why had I not come to him sooner, before mortgaging my very soul? Oh, he was kind to me." He smiled an iron smile. "He took me in his arms. He cradled my face in his hands. His baby son still. His little one. 'My little Lodovico. There are many beautiful women in the world.' That's what he said."

"This cut you to the quick," I said softly.

"Cut me? Cut me? It tore my heart as if it were food for a vulture. That's what it did to me. And what house do you think of all his many villas and houses in Rome did he plan to give to the happy bride and groom when the marriage would be accomplished?" He laughed icily and then irresistibly as if it were too funny. "The very house which he has let to Vitale to prepare for them, to air out, to furnish, and which is now the home of a noisy and evil Jewish dybbuk!"

He had changed so completely that I wouldn't have known him for the man who had been weeping in the corridor. But he fell into that daze again, hard as the lineaments of his face remained. He stared past me into the mingled trees and flowers of the courtyard. He even lifted his eyes as if he were marveling at the errant rays of the sun.

"Surely, your father understood the wound inflicted on you."

"Oh, yes," he said. "And there is another woman of immense wealth and distinction, waiting behind the inevitable curtain to make her appearance on the stage. She will be a fine wife for me, though I haven't exchanged four words with her. And my beloved Leticia will become my devoted sister when my brother rises from his bed."

"No wonder you weep," I said.

"Why do you say that?" he demanded.

"Because your soul is rent," I said. I shrugged. "How can you not watch your brother's illness without these thoughts. . . ."

"I would never wish his death!" he declared. He brought his fist down on the writing table. I thought it might crack and give way, but it did not. "No one has gone to greater lengths to save him than I. I've brought the doctors one by one to see him. I've sent for the caviar which is the only thing that he will eat."

Suddenly the old tears returned and with them a deep and genuine and exhausting pain. "I love my brother," he whispered. "I love him in all this world more than any being I have ever loved, even this woman. But I tell you there came a day when my father took me through that empty house, while Vitale and Niccolò were still in Padua, drinking themselves drunk, no doubt, and when my father took me through the place room by room to show me how very beautiful it would be and, yes, even into the bedchamber and how it would be so beautiful for them, and how and how and how!" He stopped.

"He hadn't known then."

"No. It was his secret, the name of the woman so carefully chosen. And I was the first one to bring up her name in these, these poems I wrote for her which I was fool enough, fool enough, I tell you, to reveal to him!"

"Cruel things, terribly cruel."

"Yes," he said, "and cruel things will make cruel men." He sank back in the chair, and stared before him as though he didn't know the meaning of his own story, or what it could conceivably mean to me.

"Forgive me that I've caused you this pain," I said.

"No, you require no forgiveness," he said. "The pain was in me and the pain would come out. I fear his death. I am terrified of it. I am terrified of the world without him. I am terrified of my father without him. I am terrified of Leticia without him, because she will never, never be given to me."

I wasn't sure what to make of these statements except that he meant them.

"I must get back to Vitale," I said. "He brought me here to play for your brother."

"Yes, of course. But tell me first. This tree—." He turned in his chair and looked up into the rangy green branches. He looked at the purple blossoms. "Do you know what they called it in the jungles of Brazil?"

I thought for a moment and then I said, "No. I only remember seeing it there, and I remember its blossoms and how very fragrant and beautiful they are. I should think a dye could be made from such purple blossoms."

Something changed in his face. He appeared calculating, slightly cold. I could have sworn that his mouth hardened.

I went on talking as if I hadn't noticed this, but I was beginning to dislike this man intensely.

"These blooms make me think of amethysts and there are such beautiful amethysts in Brazil."

He was silent, his eyes narrowing ever so slightly.

I couldn't bear the feeling of contempt and distrust that was growing in me. Surely I wasn't sent here to judge or to hate, but merely to prevent the man above from being poisoned.

I rose. "I should get back to Vitale," I said.

"You've been kind to me," he said, but when he smiled, only his lips moved, and it was frankly hideous. "Too bad you're a Jew."

A chill passed over me, but I held his gaze. Again, I felt that vulnerability I had known when I'd realized I was wearing the round yellow badge on my clothes. We merely looked at each other.

"Is it?" I asked. I made a small bow as if to say, I'm at your service.

He smiled again, so coldly that it was almost a grimace.

I felt the blood throbbing in my ears. I struggled to remain calm.

"Have you ever loved a woman that you couldn't have?" he asked.

I thought for a moment, unsure what to say or why to say it. I thought of Liona. I saw no point in thinking of her now, here, with this strange young man.

"I pray your brother recovers," I said suddenly, blundering, uncertain. "I pray that perhaps he'll begin to recover today. Such a thing is possible, after all. Even sick as he is, he may suddenly begin to recover."

He made a small ugly derisive sound. The smile was gone. He was looking at me now with bold hatred. And I feared I was looking at him in the same way.

He knew. He knew that I was on to him, and what he had done.

"Such a recovery could happen," I persisted. I struggled. "After all, all things are possible with God."

Again, he studied me, and this time his face was a picture of menace.

"I don't hope for that," he said, in a low iron voice. He sat upright as though gaining in strength as he spoke, "I think he will die. And if I were you, I would be gone from here before you Jews are blamed for his death. Oh, do not protest. Of course I don't suspect you of anything, but if you're wise, you'll leave Vitale to his own devices. You'll slip out of here now and go on your way."

I'd encountered many ugly and violent moments in my life. But never had I felt such menace emanating from another human being as I felt coming from him now.

What did Malchiah expect of me here? What was I to do for this man? In vain, I tried to remember Malchiah's advice to me about the difficulties I would encounter here, about the very nature of this assignment, but I couldn't recover either the words or the intent.

The fact was, I wanted to kill this man. Horrified by my own feelings, I sought to hide them. But I wanted to kill him. I wanted to grab up a handful of those lethal black seeds and force them into his mouth before he could stop me. I must have burned with the shame of it, that far from being someone's answer to a prayer, I was thinking like a very dybbuk myself. I took a deep slow breath, and made my voice as calm as I could.

"It's not too late for your brother," I said. "He might begin to mend from this very day."

There was a flash of something unnamable in his eyes, and then the rigid stillness again, the deep hostility unmasked.

"You're a fool if you remain here another moment," he whispered.

I looked down for a moment, and uttered a small wordless prayer, and when I spoke I made it as soft and gentle as I could:

"I pray your brother recovers," I said.

And then I went out.

CHAPTER SEVEN

I DREW VITALE WITH ME OUT OF THE SICKROOM AND into the passage.

"Your friend *is* being poisoned and the poison is deadly. You feed that caviar to a mongrel dog and you'll see him die before your eyes."

"But who would do this?"

"I fear to tell you: the man's own brother. But you cannot confront him. It won't be believed. This is what you must do. Instantly insist that the patient be given milk and plenty of it. Say that only white food will restore his spirits. Nothing but white food in which nothing dark has been intermixed."

"You think this will work?"

"I know it will work. The poison comes from a tree in the orangery below. It's black. It stains everything it touches black. It's the black seed of a purple flower."

"Oooh, I know this poison!" he said. "It comes from Brazil. They call it the Purple Death. I've only read of it in my manuals, and in Hebrew. I don't think it's known to the Latin doctors. I've never seen it."

"Well, I've seen it and I tell you that there is a great quantity of it growing on the tree downstairs. It's so poisonous I can't collect it without these gloves and I need a leather pouch in which to put it."

Quickly he removed a pouch from one of the pockets of his tunic, took the gold out, put this in his purse and gave me the pouch. "Here, can you safely collect it now? Will the guilty person know it when you do it?"

"Not if you keep him very busy. Call Signore Antonio. Call Lodovico. Insist they both hear you out. Say that you suspect the caviar has not helped the patient. Say that he must take milk. Say that the milk will line the stomach and absorb what evil elements are tormenting Niccolò. Say that a woman's milk is the best of all. But cow's milk will do, and goat's milk, and cheese, pure white cheese of the finest quality. The more of this you get into the patient the better. And meantime I shall take care of the poison."

"But how shall I say I came by this knowledge?"

"Say you have prayed, and you have pondered, and you have considered what has happened since the caviar was first given."

"That I have, there's no lie in that."

"Insist that the milk be tried. The loving father will see no harm in milk. No one will see harm in it. Meanwhile, I'll return to the orangery and I'll harvest as much of the poison as I can. But there's no telling how much the poisoner has already harvested himself for his purposes. I suspect not much. It's too lethal. He's been taking only the smallest doses as he needs them."

Vitale's face darkened. He shook his head. "You're telling me Lodovico has done this thing."

"I believe that he has. But what's important now is that you get the milk to your patient."

I hurried down to the small courtyard. The gates were

locked. I tried to force them very gently, but it was impossible. Nothing would have done for it but smashing the lock altogether and that I could ill afford to do.

One of the innumerable servants came up to me, a withered being whose garments appeared more like wrappings than clothes. He asked softly if he might be of help.

"Where is Signore Lodovico?" I asked, to indicate only that I'd been looking for him.

"With his father and with the priests."

"The priests?"

"Let me give you a warning," whispered this thin toothless being. "Get out of this house now while you can."

I gave him a searching look, but all he did was shake his head and walk off muttering to himself, leaving me at the locked courtyard gates. Deep inside the courtyard, I could see the bright purple flowers I had sought to harvest. I knew now there was no time for such a plan. And possibly it had not been the best plan.

As I reached Niccolò's bedchamber again, I saw approaching me Signore Antonio with two elderly priests in long black soutanes with gleaming crucifixes on their chests, and Lodovico, holding his father's arm. He was weeping again, but when he saw me, he shot me a glance as sharp as a blade.

There was no pretense of cordiality. Indeed, there was a look very like triumph on his face. And the others eyed me with obvious suspicion, though Signore Antonio himself seemed deeply troubled.

From within, I could hear Vitale ordering someone to take the caviar out. This person was arguing with him, and so was Niccolò, but I couldn't make out all that was being said.

"Young man," said Signore Antonio to me, "come in here with me now."

Two other men came behind him, and I saw that they were armed guards. They had visible daggers in their belts, and one wore a sword.

I went into the room first. It was Pico who'd been arguing with Vitale, and the caviar remained where it had been.

Niccolò lay there with his eyes half shut, and his lips dry and cracked. He sighed uneasily.

I prayed that it was not too late.

The guards slipped against the wall behind the chair where I'd been playing the lute earlier. We gathered around the bed.

Signore Antonio eyed me for a long moment and then he stared at Vitale. As for Lodovico, he had given way to tears again, very convincingly, as before.

"Wake up, my son," said Signore Antonio. "Wake up, and hear the truth from your brother's lips. I fear it can no longer be avoided, and only in the telling of it can the disaster be averted."

"What is this, Father?" asked the patient. He seemed weaker than ever, though the caviar sat still where we had left it.

"Speak," said Signore Antonio to Lodovico.

The young man faltered, wiped at his tears with a silk handkerchief and then said, "I have no choice but to reveal that Vitale, our trusted friend, our confidant, our companion, has in fact bewitched my brother!"

Niccolò sat up with more strength than I'd ever witnessed.

"How dare you say such a thing? You know my friend is incapable of this. Bewitched me how and to what purpose?"

Lodovico gave way to a fresh shower of tears and appealed to his father with open arms.

"Unbeknownst to me, my son," said Antonio, "this man has craved to keep the house in which he lives, the house in which I let him live while you were ill, the house which I had chosen to bestow on you and your bride. He has summoned the evil spirit there to do his bidding, and it is by means of this evil spirit that he has made you gravely ill, and hopes that you will die so that the house may be his. He has prayed for this to his God. He has prayed for this, and Lodovico has heard his prayers."

"This is a lie. I prayed for no such thing," said Vitale. "I live in the house at your pleasure, and seek to put the old library in order, at your pleasure, and to find what Hebrew manuscripts were left behind years ago by the man who left the house to you. But I have never prayed for an evil spirit to aid me in any way, and would never have such evil designs upon my closest friend."

He stared at Signore Antonio in disbelief. "How can you accuse me of this? You think that in hopes of a palazzo I can well afford to buy I would sacrifice the life of my closest friend in all the world? Signore, you wound me as if with a knife."

Signore Antonio listened to this, as if his mind was not made up.

"Do you not have a synagogue within this house?" demanded the taller of the two priests, who was obviously the elder. He was a man of dark gray hair and sharpened features. But his face was not cruel. "Do you not have the Scrolls of your Torah in that synagogue set into an Ark?"

"These things are there, yes," said Vitale. "They were there when I took the house. It's general knowledge that a Jew lived there, and he has left these things, and for twenty years they've been layered in dust."

At this Signore Antonio seemed particularly affected. But he didn't speak.

"You've never used these things in your evil prayers?" demanded the second priest, a more timid man, but one who was now trembling with ill-concealed excitement.

"Well, I must confess in all truth I have not used them in

my prayers," said Vitale. "I must confess I'm more the humanist, the poet, the physician, than I am the pious Jew. Forgive me, but I have not used them. I've gone to the synagogue of my friends for my Sabbath prayers, and you know those men, you know them well, they're respected by all of you."

"Ah," said the tall priest. "So you admit you uttered no holy or pious prayers to these strange books, and yet we are to assume they are your sacred books and not some strange and foreign books of secrets and enchantments?"

"Do you deny you have such things?" asked the younger priest.

"Why do you accuse me of this!" Vitale said. "Signore Antonio, I love you. I love Niccolò. I love his bride-to-be as if she were my sister. You have been to me since Padua as my very family."

Signore Antonio was clearly shaken, but he stood up straight as if these accusations required all his resolve.

"Vitale, speak the truth to me," he said. "Have you bewitched my son? Have you said over him strange incantations? Have you made vows to the Evil One that you would offer up to him this Christian death for some dark purpose of your own?"

"Never, never have I uttered a syllable of prayer to the Evil One," said Vitale.

"Then why is my son in this sickened state? Why does he fail day in and day out? Why is he troubled in this way, while a demon roars in your house this very minute, as if he is waiting to see how well you can work your dark charms for him?"

"Lodovico, is this your doing?" Vitale demanded. "Did you put this in the minds of all these who are present?"

"Allow me to speak," I said. "I'm a stranger to you all, but not a stranger to the cause of your son's ailment."

"And who are you that we should listen to you?" demanded the elder priest.

"A world traveler, a student of natural things, of plants and obscure flowers and even of poisons so as to find some cure for them."

"Silence!" said Lodovico. "You dare interject yourself here in this family matter. Father, order this musician out of the room. He's no more than a henchman to Vitale."

"Not so, Signore," said Vitale. "This man has taught me much." He turned to me and I could see the fear in his face, the general suspicion that perhaps the things I'd told him were not true, and now everything hung upon their being true.

"Signore," I said to the old man. "You see the caviar there."

"From the Pope's palace!" declared Lodovico. He then went into a stream of words to silence me. But I persisted. "You see it there!" I said. "It's black, salty to the taste. You know full well what it is. Well, I assure you, sir, that if you were to eat four or five spoonfuls of it, you would soon be pale and sweating as your son is, and white as he is as well. In fact, a man of your age might well die altogether from that amount of it."

The priests both stared at the little silver dish of caviar and both backed away from it instinctively.

"Signore," I went on. "In your orangery, off the main courtyard below, there is a plant known to the Brazilians as Purple Death. I tell you just one of its black seeds is enough to sicken a man. A steady diet of them, ground up and placed in a pungent food such as that, would very surely kill him."

"I don't believe you!" whispered the old man. "Who would do this?"

"You lie," cried Lodovico, "you tell fantastic lies to protect your cohort and who knows what sins you're guilty of together."

"Then eat the caviar," I said. "Eat not just one small spoon of it, as you try to feed to your brother, but eat all of it, and we shall see if the truth doesn't come out. And if that is not sufficient, I will take you all down and reveal the plant to you, and reveal its powers. Find a pitiful mongrel in the streets of Rome and feed him the seeds of this plant and you'll see him quiver and shake and die immediately."

Lodovico drew his dagger from out of his sleeve.

At once the priests shouted for him to be still, to restrain himself, not to be foolish.

"You need a dagger to eat the food?" I said. "Just take the silver spoon. You'll find it easier."

"These are lies that this man tells," cried Lodovico, "and who under this roof, who would do such a thing to my brother? Who would dare! And this caviar has come from the kitchen of the Holy Father himself. This is vile, I tell you."

A silence fell as if someone had rung a bell.

Signore Antonio stared at his natural son who still faced me with his drawn dagger. I stood as before, the lute slung over my back, merely looking at him. As for Vitale, he was white and shaken and on the verge of tears.

"Why did you plot this thing?" Signore Antonio asked in a soft voice, his question clearly aimed at Lodovico.

"I plotted no such thing. And there is no such plant."

"Oh, but there is," said Signore Antonio. "And you brought it into this house. I remember it. I remember its unmistakable purple flowers."

"A gift for us from those dear kindred of ours in Brazil," said Lodovico. He appeared wounded. He appeared sad. "A beautiful blossom for a garden of beautiful blossoms. I made no effort to conceal this plant from you. I know nothing of its powers. Who does know of its powers?" He looked at me. "You!" he said to me, "and your fellow Jew, Vitale, your fellow cohort in this plot. Are you worshippers of the Evil One together! Did the Evil One tell you what this plant could do? If this caviar is tainted, it's with the poison you both put into it." His wonderful copious tears were flowing again. "How vile of you to do this to my brother."

Signore Antonio shook his head. His eyes were fixed on Lodovico. "No," he whispered. "Neither man could have done this thing. You brought the plant. You brought the caviar into the house."

"Father, they are witches, these men. They are evil."

"Are they?" asked Signore Antonio. "And what friend of ours from Brazil sent us this unusual flower? Rather, I think you purchased it in this very city, and brought it home and placed it very near the table where you do your writings, your translations."

"No, a gift, I tell you. I don't recall now when it came."

"But I do. And it was only a short time ago, and at the very same time that you, my son, Lodovico, hit upon the idea that caviar would sharpen the attitude of your weakened brother."

All this while the patient had watched these proceedings with horror. He'd glanced to the left at his father, to the right at his brother, he'd studied the priests when they spoke. He'd stared at me with piercing horrified eyes as I spoke.

And now he leaned forward and picked up the bowl of caviar in his quivering hand.

"No, don't touch it!" I said. "Don't let it near your eyes. It will burn them. Don't you remember this?"

"I remember it," said the father.

One of the priests reached for the dish, but the patient had set it down on the mount of brocade coverlets, and he stared at it, as if it had a life of its own, as if he were looking at the flame of a candle.

He lifted the small spoon in his hand.

His father suddenly seized it from him and threw the caviar to the side where it fell on the coverlet and stained it black.

Lodovico, before he could check himself, moved back from the bed where the caviar had spilled. He stepped backwards instinctively. And only then did he realize what he'd done. He looked up at his father.

He still held the dagger in his hand.

"You think me guilty of this?" he demanded of his father. "There is no poison there, I tell you. There is nothing but a stain now which the washerwomen will seek in vain to wash out. But there is no poison."

"Come with me," I said, "down to the orangery. I'll show you the tree. Find some hapless animal. I'll show you what this poison can do. I'll show you how very black it is, this seed, and how perfect was the caviar for concealing it."

Suddenly Lodovico rushed at me with the dagger. I knew well how to defend myself, and smashed the hard side of my hand into his wrist, knocking the blade out of his grip, but then he went for my throat with outstretched fingers. I brought my arms up instantly crossed, and struck out, forcing his arms apart with a wild and sudden gesture.

He fell back confounded by these simple moves. Neither of them would have been much of a surprise in our times when martial arts are taught to children. I was ashamed of how much I had enjoyed the struggle.

One of the guards picked up the dagger.

Lodovico stood shaken, and then, desperately, he ran his hand along the stain on the coverlet, gathering up but a few grains of the caviar and he put this on his tongue. "See, I tell you, I am maligned. I am maligned by evil Jews who consort to destroy me for no other reason but that I know their tricks and what they would have done to Niccolò."

He licked his lips. He'd had but the tiniest portion of the caviar, and could easily conceal the effects.

Again a deep silence fell. Only the sudden shuddering of Niccolò broke the silence.

"Brother," he whispered. "This is all on account of Leticia."

"A lie!" said Lodovico thickly. "How dare you?"

"Oh, if only I'd known," said Niccolò. "What is she but one of many lovely young maidens who might have been to me a gentle bride? If only I'd known."

Signore Antonio glowered at Lodovico.

"Leticia, is it?" he whispered.

"I tell you, these Jews have bewitched him. I tell you it is they who put the poison in the caviar, I tell you I am innocent." He was weeping, he was angry, he was whispering and muttering, and once again, he spoke. "It was this one, Vitale, who brought the flower to the house. I remember it now. How else should he and his friend know of its power? I tell you, this one, this Toby, is convicted out of his own mouth."

The old man shook his head at the pity of it.

"Come," said Signore Antonio. He gestured for his armed servants to take Lodovico in hand. He looked at me. "Take me down to the orangery and show me this medicine."

CHAPTER EIGHT

THE YOUNG MAN'S FACE WAS TWISTED WITH MALICE. The very plasticity which had given him such easy grief before now gave him a mask of fury. He pushed the armed men off and walked with his head high as we descended the steps, and gathered, all of us, save for Niccolò, of course, in the orangery.

There stood the plant, and I pointed out the many black seeds which had fallen already into the soil. I pointed out the half-withered flowers already harboring the poison.

A servant was sent to find some poor stray dog that it might be brought into the house, and soon the yelps of the poor little beast were echoing up the broad stairway.

Vitale stared at the purple flowers in horror. Signore Antonio merely glowered at it, and the two priests stood staring coldly at me and at Vitale as though we were still somehow responsible for what had happened here.

An elderly woman, much bewildered and frightened, produced a crockery dish for the poor starved dog and went to fill it with water.

I put back on the gloves I'd removed to play the lute, and requesting Lodovico's dagger, I gathered the seeds into a heap and then looked around for something with which to crush them. Only the handle of the dagger was at hand. And so I used it to make a powder, a good pinch of which I now put into the dog's water. I put in another pinch and yet another.

The animal drank thirstily and miserably and licked at the bare dish and then immediately began to twitch. It fell on its side, and then on its back and writhed in its agony. In a moment, it had become rigid, its eyes staring dully at nothing and no one.

All watched this little spectacle with revulsion and horror, including me.

But Lodovico was incensed, staring at the priests, and at his father, and then at the dog.

"I swear I am innocent of this!" he declared. "The Jews know the poison. The Jews brought it here. Why, it was this very Jew Vitale who brought the plant to the house . . ."

"You contradict your story," said Antonio. "You lie. You stammer. You beg for credence like a coward!"

"I tell you I had no part in it!" cried out the desperate man. "These Jews have bewitched me as they have bewitched my brother. If this thing was done by me, it was in a sleep in which I knew nothing. It was in a sleep in which I wandered, carrying out the acts they forced me to carry out. What do you know of these Jews? You speak of their holy books, but what do you know of these books but that they aren't filled with the witchcraft that drove me to this? Doesn't the demon rage in the accursed house at this very hour?"

"Signore Antonio," said the elder priest, the one with the sharp yet gentle features. "Something must be said of this demon. People in the street can hear it howl. Is all this beyond what a demon can do? I think not!"

Lodovico had a thousand protests—that yes, it was the demon, and yes, it had worked its sinister magic on him, and could no one imagine the evil of this demon, and so forth and so on.

But the solemn Antonio was having none of it. He stared at his natural son with a face that was sad to the point of tears, but no tears flowed. "How could you do this?" he whispered.

Suddenly Lodovico broke loose from the two men who stood beside him, their hands barely holding him.

He rushed at the tree of purple flowers and grabbed at the black seeds in the mud of the pot. He caught as many as his hand could hold.

"Stop him," I cried. And I flew at him, pushing him backwards, but his hand shot to his lips before I could stop it, forcing the mud and seeds into his open mouth. I jerked his hand away but it was too late.

The guards were on him and so was his father.

"Make him vomit it up," cried Vitale desperately. "Let me get to him, stand back."

But I knew it was useless.

I moved away, utterly distraught. What had I allowed to happen here! It was too awful. It was exactly what I myself had wanted to do to him, what I myself had pictured, scooping up the seeds, forcing him to eat them, but he had done this himself as if my evil intentions had taken hold of him. How had I let him do this dreadful deed? Why had I not figured some way to turn him from his purpose?

Lodovico looked at his father. He was choking and shuddering. The guards backed away and only Signore Antonio held him as he began to convulse and then to slip to the floor.

"Merciful Lord," whispered Signore Antonio, and so did I.

Merciful Lord, have mercy on his immortal soul. Lord in Heaven, forgive him his madness.

"Witchcraft!" said the dying man, his mouth smeared with

saliva and mud, and it was his last word. On his knees, he bent forward, his face contorted, and the convulsions shook his entire frame.

Then he rolled over on his side, his legs still twitching, and his face took on the rigid grimace of the poor animal that had died before him.

And I, I who in a life hundreds of years away, and in a land far far away, had used this very poison to dispatch untold victims, could only stand staring helplessly at this one. Oh, what a blunder, that I, sent to answer prayers, had brought about a suicide.

A silence fell over us all.

"He was my friend," Vitale whispered.

As the old man started to rise, Vitale took his arm.

Niccolò appeared in the gateway. Not making a sound, he stood there in his long white bed tunic, barefoot, trembling, yet staring at his dead brother.

"Go out, all of you," said Signore Antonio. "Leave me with my son here. Leave me."

But the elder priest lingered. He was much shaken as were we all, but he gathered his resources and said in a low, contemptuous voice,

"Do not think for a moment that witchcraft is not in operation here," he said. "That your sons have not been contaminated by their intercourse with these Jews."

"Fr. Piero, silence," said the old man. "This was not witchcraft, this was envy! And I did not see what I did not want to see. Now leave me, all of you. Leave me to be alone to mourn my son whom I took from his mother's arms. Vitale, take your patient to his bed. He will recover now."

"But the demon, does it not still rage?" the priest demanded. No one was listening to him.

I stared down at the dead man. I couldn't speak. Couldn't think. I knew they were all going out, except for the old man, and I must go out as well. Yet I couldn't take my eyes off his lifeless body. I thought of angels, but without words. I appealed to an unseen realm, intermingled with our own, beings of wisdom and compassion who might be surrounding the soul of this dead man now, but no comforting images came to mind, no words. I had failed. I had failed this one, though I might have saved another. Was that all I had been meant to do? Save the one brother and drive the other to destroy himself? It was inconceivable. And it was I who had driven him to this, most certainly.

I looked up and saw old Pico in the gateway gesturing for me to hurry. All the others had gone out.

I bowed and went behind Signore Antonio and out of the orangery, and into the larger courtyard.

I was dazed. I think perhaps Fr. Piero was there, but I didn't really look at those standing about.

I saw the open doorway to the street, with the dim silhouettes of a couple of servants keeping watch there, and I moved towards the door and then went through it.

No one questioned me. No one seemed to notice me.

I walked numbly into the crowded piazza and for one moment stared up at the darkening grayish sky. How perfectly solid and real was this world into which I'd been plunged, with its crowded stone houses, built slap against one another, and their random towers. How real the walls of the palazzos opposite, somber and brown, and how real the noises of this motley crowd, with their carefree conversation, and bursts of laughter.

Where was I going? What did I mean to do? I wanted to pray, to go into a church and fall on my knees and pray, yet how could I do this with the yellow patch on my clothes? How could I dare to make the Sign of the Cross, without someone thinking I was mocking my own faith?

I felt lost and knew only that I was wandering away from the houses to which I'd been sent. And when I thought of the soul of the dead man, going now to the utter unknown, I was desperate.

CHAPTER NINE

I STOPPED. I FOUND MYSELF IN A NARROW MUDDY LANE, overcome with the stench of the filth flowing into the gutters. I thought again of trying to reach a church, a place where I could go down on my knees in the shadows and pray to God for help with this, but then again the thought of the round yellow badge on the left side of my chest stopped me.

People passed me on both sides, some politely giving me room, others shouldering me out of their path, while others milled at the open cookshops and bakery shops. The fragrances of roasting meat and baked bread mingled with the stench.

I felt suddenly too weak in spirit to go further, and finding a narrow margin of wall between a fabric merchant's open stall and a bookseller, I slipped my lute around into my arms, and then holding it like a baby, I leaned back and rested and tried to find above the narrow margin of the sky.

The light was dying fast. It was getting chilly. Lamps burned in the shops. A torchbearer made his way through the street with two smartly dressed young men behind him.

I realized I had no idea what month of the year it was here, and if it corresponded in some way to the late spring weather I'd left behind. But the Mission Inn, and my beloved Liona, seemed utterly remote, like something I'd dreamed.

That I'd ever been Lucky the Fox, a paid assassin, seemed unreal as well.

Again, I prayed for Lodovico's soul. But the words seemed meaningless suddenly, in the face of my failure, and then I heard a voice say very close to me,

"You don't have to wear that badge."

Before I could look up, I felt the badge being ripped from the velvet of my tunic. I saw a tall young man standing there, dressed very well in brilliant burgundy velvet, with dark hose and black boots. He wore a sword in a heavily jeweled scabbard, and a short cloak over his shoulders of gray velvet as fine as that of his tunic.

He had long hair, much like my own, but it was a soft brown in color, very lustrous and curled just as it touched his shoulders. His face was remarkably symmetrical and his full mouth very beautiful. He had large dark brown eyes.

In the gloved fingers of his right hand, he held the round yellow badge that he'd so easily ripped from its stitches, and he crumpled it up now, as best he could, and tucked it into his belt.

"You don't need it," he said in the most gentle confidential way. "You're Vitale's servant and he and all his household and family are exempt from wearing the badge. He should have thought to tell you to take it off."

"But why, what does it matter?" I asked.

He lifted a short red velvet cape that he'd been carrying over his left arm and he put it over my shoulders. He then put a sword on me, buckling the belt into place. I stared at it. At the jeweled handle.

"What is all this?" I asked. "Who are you?"

"It's time you had a little rest, and time to think," he said in the same soft confidential voice. "I'm to take you away from here for a while, to give you some time for reflection."

He took my arm. I slung the lute over my back again and let him lead me out of this alley.

It was now almost completely dark. Torches were passing us, making a spitting sound as they flared, and some of the shops now poured their light into the narrow walkway. I couldn't quite see for the glare of the lights.

"Who sent you to me?" I asked.

"Who do you think?" he answered. He had slipped his arm around me, under the lute, and he was pressing me gently forward. His body seemed immaculately clean and smelled faintly of a dark sweet perfume.

The others I'd encountered here had not by any means been dirty, but even the best of them had a slightly dusty appearance and some smell of natural skin and hair.

This man gave off nothing of the sort.

"But what about Vitale?" I asked. "It's all right to leave him at such a time?"

"Nothing will happen tonight," the man assured me, looking directly into my eyes as he bent slightly towards me. "They'll bury Lodovico, and it won't be in consecrated ground, of course, but the father will accompany the body to the site. The household will mourn, whether it is permitted to mourn a suicide or not."

"But that priest, Fr. Piero, what about his accusations, and I don't know whether the dybbuk is still raging."

"Why don't you put yourself in my hands," he said, as gently as if he were a physician, "and let me heal the pain you're feeling? Let me suggest that you're in no state to help anyone just now. You need to be refreshed."

We walked through another huge piazza. Torches blazed at the entrances of the immense four-storied houses, and lights shone in myriad towers against the dark blue sky. A sprinkling of stars was visible.

I saw that men around me were very ornately dressed, flashing ringed fingers, or bright colored gloves, and many were hurrying in groups as if to an important destination.

Women in lavish silk and brocade made their way daintily through the dust, their drably dressed servants hurrying to catch up with them. Finely decorated litters passed, the bearers trotting under their burden, the passengers concealed behind brightly colored curtains. I could hear music in the distance, but the noise of voices swallowed it up.

I wanted to stop and take in all of this ever-shifting spectacle, but I was uneasy.

"Why didn't Malchiah come to me?" I asked. "Why did he send you?"

The brown-haired man smiled and, looking at me lovingly as if I were a child in his care, he said, "Never mind about Malchiah. You will forgive me a little mocking tone when we speak of him, won't you? The powerful ones are always mocked a little by the less powerful." His eyes flashed with good humor. "Come, this is the Cardinal's palazzo. The banquet has been going on since this afternoon."

"What cardinal?" I whispered. "Who is he?"

"Does it matter? This is Rome in an age of splendor, and what have you seen of it, so far? Nothing but the dreary goings-on of one miserable household?"

"Wait a moment, I don't . . ."

"Come now, it's time to learn," he said. And again it was as if he were talking to a small child. I found this both attractive and extremely off-putting. "You know what you've been longing to see all this time," he went on, "and there are things that you should see here because they are a glorious part of this world."

His voice had a rich resonance to it, and it seemed he was thinking of these things naturally as he spoke. Not even

Malchiah's smile had this quality of tenderness to it. Or so it seemed in the brightening light.

We fell into a veritable stream of lavishly dressed company, and entered beneath a huge gilded archway into what might have been an enormous courtyard or hall, I could not tell which. Hundreds of people were milling about.

On the margins of this space were tall stately evergreens decked with candles, and just before us an endless row of heavily draped tables stretching out to the right and the left.

Some guests were already seated including a company in rich robes and caps, their faces toward the great open space beyond the tables where any number of male servants were coming and going with wineskins, trays of goblets, and platters of what appeared to be gilded fruit.

High above us were great painted wooden arches garlanded with flowers, and supporting an endless canopy of shimmering silver cloth.

Torches flared on the margins of the room. And heavy golden and silver candelabra were being placed every few feet along the tables, together with golden plates. People were taking their seats on cushioned benches.

I was led to the far right where several men were already seated, and we quickly took our places. I found it awkward handling the sword. I placed my lute safely at my feet.

The place was now swarming with guests.

There must have been over a thousand. Everywhere the women were a feast for the eye with their bare white shoulders and scantily covered breasts, in deeply colored gowns with slashed sleeves, and ropes of pearls and gems in their elaborately done hair. But the younger men seemed equally as interesting, with their lustrous long hair, and brightly colored hose. Their slashed sleeves were as ornate as those of the women, and they wore an infinite variety of colors as well. The men were preening, more boldly than the women, but a contagious goodwill seem to unite all.

Suddenly, a troop of boys appeared, dressed in flimsy belted tunics, obviously intended to evoke ancient Greek or Roman tastes. Their arms and legs were bare, and they wore gilded sandals, and garlands of leaves and blossoms in their hair.

Surely their cheeks had been rouged, and maybe some paint applied as well to darken their eyes. They laughed and smiled and murmured easily, filling goblets and offering plates of candies, as though they'd been doing this sort of thing all their young lives.

One of these lithe little Ganymedes filled the silver goblets in front of us from a huge wineskin that he handled deftly as though he'd done this a thousand times.

Far to the right of us, a group of musicians had begun to play, and it seemed the voices around me grew louder, as if excited by the music. The music itself was uncommonly lovely, with a rich melody rising, a melody that sounded familiar to me but which really wasn't, played by viols, lutes and horns. Surely there were other instruments, but I didn't know what they were. Another group of musicians far to my left joined the first in the very same song. A slow rhythmic drumbeat underscored the melody, and other melodies became interwound with it, until I lost track of the structure of the music altogether. I could feel the beating of the drums against my ears.

I was enthralled by all of this, but I was also disturbed. My eyes were watering as much from perfume as from candle wax.

"Malchiah wants me to do this," I pressed. I reached out and touched the young man's right wrist. "He wants that I attend this banquet?"

"Do you think he would allow it if he didn't want it?" the man answered with the most innocent expression. "Here, drink. You've been here almost a full day and you haven't tasted the delicious wine of Italy." He smiled again that very sweet and loving smile, as he put my goblet in my hand.

I was about to protest that I never drank, couldn't even bear the smell of it, when I realized this wasn't really entirely true, just a matter of policy, and the delicious aroma of the wine was rising with a remarkable seductive power. I took the goblet and tasted it. It was the way I loved it, dry and with a slight smoky flavor, and as good a wine as I'd ever had. I took another drink of it, and a soothing warmth moved through me. Who was I to question what the angels wanted? All around me people were feasting from golden plates, and chattering comfortably with one another, and as a third group of musicians joined the other ensembles, I felt myself yielding to this, as if to a dream.

"Here, drink again," said my companion. He pointed to a slender blond woman who was just passing us in the company of several older persons, a vision with her yellow hair done up in white flowers and brilliant jewels.

"That is the young woman who caused all the trouble," he said to me, "your Leticia, whom Lodovico so coveted, though she is promised to Niccolò, who almost lost his life." His tone was almost reverent but something about his choice of words disturbed me and I might have said something about it, but he offered me my own goblet again.

I drank. And I drank again.

My head swam. I shut my eyes and opened them again, seeing at first nothing but myriad candles blazing everywhere, and only now did I see there were tables under the arches all down both sides of this grand space. They were as crowded as we were here.

One of the boys refilled my cup, and smiled warmly at me as he moved away. I drank again. Slowly my head cleared. Everywhere I looked I saw color and movement. People were moving out of the open space before us, and the music grew louder, and quite suddenly two trumpets sounded, to a great outbreak of applause.

Into the open space before us came a troupe of dancers, brilliantly costumed to suggest classical gods and goddesses, in gilded armor and helmets, with shields and spears, and they performed for us now a kind of slow, graceful and careful ballet. People were applauding eagerly, and the chatter everywhere increased in volume again.

I could have watched these languid dancers forever as they made their careful circles and turns, and formations. Suddenly the music picked up, the dancers moved away, and a lute player came to the fore, and placing one foot on a small silver stool, he proceeded to sing loudly but gracefully in Latin of the varieties of love.

A kind of dizziness came over me, but I felt warm and supremely comfortable and dazzled by what I saw before me. The lute player was gone. There were actors again, some got up as horses, and they were acting a battle scene with much noise and frequent rounds of applause.

There was food on the gold plate in front of me, and indeed I realized I'd been eating it rather eagerly, when the servants came to remove our dishes and to remove the tablecloth to reveal another cloth, of crimson and gold, underneath.

Bowls of scented water were being passed for us to wash our hands.

The first course had been taken away and I'd scarcely noticed it, and now came the servants with platters of roasted fowl and steaming vegetables. And we were once again piling the food on our plates. There were no forks, but that didn't surprise me. We ate with our fingers and with the aid of gold knives. Again and again, I drank as the boys refilled our goblets, and my eyes were drawn back to the area before me when a great painted backdrop of streets and buildings was wheeled noisily into place, transforming the flagstones into a more elaborate stage.

I couldn't make out the subject of the drama that followed. I was distracted by the undercurrent of music, and finally just too sleepy to pay much attention to any one beautiful thing.

Another round of applause drew me out of my daze. Suckling pigs were being brought in now and the aroma was overpowering, though I did not want to eat anymore.

A sudden alarm brought me to my senses. What was I doing? Why was I here? I'd meant to grieve and mourn for Lodovico and my own failure to save him, yet I was banqueting with strangers, and laughing with them at lavish theatricals that made little or no sense to me at all.

I wanted to speak but the man who'd brought me here was talking with the one next to him, and saying in the most earnest voice. "Do it. Do what you want to do. You will do it, anyway, won't you? So why torture yourself about it, or about anything, for that matter?"

He stared forward and drank from his cup.

"You didn't tell me your name," I said, touching his sleeve.

He turned and flashed one of his tenderest smiles at me. "It has too many syllables," he said, "and you have no need to know it."

The meat was being offered to us. He cut a large piece from the platter and put it on my plate. With a giant gold spoon he scooped up the rice and the cabbage and gave me a helping of this as well.

"No, no more," I said. "I must leave, actually. I have to get back."

"Oh, nonsense, you mustn't. They'll be dancing soon, for everyone. And then more entertainment. The evening's only just begun. These celebrations go on all night." He pointed to a group at the distant tables that flanked the right side of the hall. "See there, those are guests of the Cardinal from Venice. He's doing his very best to impress them."

"That's all fine and good," I said. "But I have to see what's happened to Vitale. I think I've been here too long."

I heard a lovely light riff of laughter near me, and I turned to see that incomparably beautiful Leticia bending her head towards the man beside her. "Surely she doesn't know that Niccolò has lost his brother," I said.

"No, of course, she doesn't," said my companion. "Do you think the family is going to publicize the disgrace, that the idiot took his own life? They're burying him and leave them alone to do it. Let them do their sneaking off by themselves."

I felt a cold anger come over me. "Why do you talk of them like that?" I asked. "They're suffering, all of them, and I'm here to help them in their suffering, I'm here as an answer to their prayers. You sound as if you don't approve of them or their prayers!"

I realized I'd raised my voice. It seemed brazen. I was confused. Was I talking to an angel?

He stared at me, and I got lost suddenly in studying his face. His eyebrows were high placed and dark and straight, and his eyes themselves very large and clear. His mouth was soft, full and smiling as though he thought me entertaining, but he didn't seem scornful or disdainful at all.

"Are you the answer to their prayers?" he asked gently. He seemed so very concerned. "Are you? Do you really think that is why you're here?" He seemed to be speaking very softly, too softly for this immense place, and too softly to be heard over that urgent and beautiful music coming from both sides of the hall. But I could hear every word he said.

"What if I told you that you were not the answer to anyone's prayer, that you were the dupe of spirits who would have you believe this for reasons of their own?" He appeared worried, and he laid his warm hand on my left wrist.

I was terrified. I said nothing. I just looked at him, at the soft thick waves of his long hair, at his steady eyes. I wasn't terrified of him, but of what he had just said. If that was so, the world was meaningless and I was lost. I felt it keenly and instantly.

"What are you saying?" I asked.

"That you've been lied to," he offered with the same tender solicitude. "There are no angels, Toby, there are only spirits, discarnate spirits and the spirits of those who've been alive in the flesh and are no longer alive in the flesh. You weren't sent here to help anybody. The spirits who are manipulating you are feeding off your emotions, feeding as surely as the people in this room are feeding off these plates."

He seemed desperate to make me understand this. I could have sworn tears were coming to his eyes.

"Malchiah didn't send you here, did he? You have nothing to do with him," I said.

"Of course, he didn't send me, but you must ask yourself why he can't stop me from telling you the truth."

"I don't believe you," I said. I tried to rise, but he held fast to my arm.

"Toby, don't go. Don't turn away from the truth. My time with you may be shorter than I hoped. Let me assure you, you're locked in a belief system that is nothing but the stage machinery of lies."

"No," I said. "I don't know who you are, but I won't listen to this."

"Why not? Why does it make you so afraid? I've come here out of time to try to warn you against this superstitious belief in angels and gods and devils. Now let me please try to reach your heart."

"Why would you do this?" I asked.

"There are many discarnate entities like me in the universe," he said. "We try to guide souls like you who are lost in the belief systems. We try to urge you back on the path of real spiritual growth. Toby, your soul can be trapped in a belief system like this for centuries, don't you realize it?"

"How did I get here, how did I travel back five centuries in time if this is all a lie?" I demanded. "Let go of me. I am going to leave."

"Five centuries back in time?" He laughed the softest, saddest laugh. "Toby, you haven't traveled back in time, you're in another dimension, that's all, one your spirit masters have constructed for you because it suits them as they harvest your emotions and those of the beings around you for their own pleasure."

"Stop saying this," I said. "It's a ghastly idea. You think I haven't heard such ideas before?"

I was afraid. I was shocked and afraid. My intellect rebelled at every word he'd spoken but I was shaken. A cold terror might get the upper hand in me at any moment.

"The terms you're using, they aren't new to me," I said. "You don't think I've read theories of multiple dimensions, stories of souls who travel out of body, who find earthbound spirits trapped in realities they need to escape?"

"Well, if you've read these things, for the love of yourself and all you hold dear, question these awful beings who are manipulating you!" he insisted. "Break free of them. You can get out of this grotesque trap, this elaborate bubble in time and space, simply by willing it."

"By what!" I scoffed. "Clicking my heels and saying 'There's no place like home'? Look, I don't know who you are but I know what you're trying to do, you're trying to prevent me from getting back to Vitale, for doing what I've come here to do. And your urgency, my friend, does more to undercut your anemic theories than my logic can do."

He seemed heartbroken.

"You're right," he confessed, his eyes gleaming, "I am trying to deter you, to turn you back to your own growth and your own capacity to seek the truth. Toby, don't you want the truth? You know the things this so-called angel told you were nothing but lies. There is no Supreme Being listening to anyone's prayers. There are no winged angels sent to implement His will." His mouth lengthened in a sneer. But then his face formed the expression of utter compassion again.

"Why in the world should I believe you?" I asked. "Yours is an empty universe, an implausible universe, and I rejected it a long time ago. I rejected it when my hands were bloody and my soul black. I rejected it because it made no sense to me, and it makes no sense to me now. Why is this belief system of yours more plausible than mine?"

"Believe, believe, believe, I ask that you use your reason," he pleaded. "Listen, your spirit bullies may be back at any moment to collect you. Please, I beg you, trust in what I have to say. You are a powerful spiritual being, Toby, and you don't need a jealous god who demands worship, or his angel henchmen sending you to answer prayers!"

"And for whom did you come here, and with so much passion, and so much effort?"

"I told you. I'm one of many discarnate entities sent to help you in your journey. Toby, this is the lowest and most draining sort of belief system, this miserable religion of yours. You must get beyond this if you are ever to evolve."

"You were sent, sent by whom?"

"How can I make you understand?" He seemed genuinely sad. "You've lived many lives, but always with one soul."

"I've heard that one a million times."

"Toby, look into my eyes. I'm the personality of a life you once lived long ago."

"You make me laugh," I said.

His eyes filled with tears. "Toby, I am the man you were in this time, don't you see, and I've come to awaken you to what the universe truly is. It has nothing to do with Heaven or Hell. There are no gods demanding worship. There is no good or evil. These are constructs. You've fallen into a trap that makes spiritual growth impossible. Challenge these beings. Refuse to obey."

"No," I said. Something changed in me. The fear was gone, and the anger I'd felt was gone. A calm came over me, and once again I was conscious of the music, of that same lovely melody playing that I had heard when I first came. There was something so eloquent of justice and beauty in the music, so expressive of a virtue that it could break one's heart.

I turned and looked at the assemblage. People were dancing, men and women in circles, holding hands, one circle revolving one way, the outer circle another.

His voice came right by my ear. "You are beginning to think about it, aren't you?"

"I've thought about it, the ideas you're offering. As I told you, I've heard them before." I turned and looked at him. "But I don't see anything convincing in your argument. As I said, you are describing a belief system of your own. What proof have you that there are other dimensions, or that there is no God?"

"I don't have to have proof of what is not," he said. He appeared distraught. "I appeal to your common sense. You've lived many times, Toby," he said, "and many times spirits like me have come to help you, and sometimes you've taken that help, and sometimes not. You come back into the flesh over and over again with a plan to learn certain things, and your learning cannot progress if you don't realize that this is so."

"No, it's a belief system all right, everything you're saying, and like all belief systems it presents a certain coherence and a certain beauty, but I rejected it long ago. I told you, I find it empty and I do."

"How can you say such a thing?"

"Do you really want to know? Do you really truly want to know?"

"I love you. I am you. I'm here to help you move on."

"I know because deep in my soul, I know there is a God. There is someone I love whom I call God. That someone has emotions. That someone is Love. And I sense the presence of this God in the very fabric of the world in which I live. I know with a deep conviction that this God exists. That He would send angels to His children has an elegance to it that I can't deny. I've studied your ideas, your system, as it were, and I find it barren and finally unconvincing, and cold. Finally it's dreadfully cold. It's without the personality of God and it's cold."

"No," he protested, shaking his head. "It's not cold. I'm pleading with you. You're wrong. You're putting a god at the center of your system that never existed. Only the child in you insists on this god. That child must yield to the man."

I got up from the table, bringing the lute with me. I stopped, unbuckled the sword and let it drop to the floor. I let go of the cloak he'd given me when we met.

Suddenly my head began to spin.

"Don't go, Toby," he said.

He was standing next to me. No. We were walking together through the milling crowd. I was dizzy. Someone pushed a goblet of wine at me, and I waved it away.

He threw his arms around me and tried to stop me.

"Let me go, I warn you," I said. "I do not care for what you've offered me. I don't know whether you're evil or simply lost on some journey of your own. But I know what I have to do. I have to return to Vitale and help him in any way I can."

"You can be free," he whispered, his face very close to mine. "Defy them, curse them!" he said, his face reddening. "Denounce them and repudiate them. They have no right to use you." His whisper had become a hiss.

He glanced from right to left. He released me but then placed his hands tightly on my shoulders, and I could feel the pressure of his fingers growing very strong.

I hated this. It was all I could do not to hit him and try to knock him aside.

"Will you believe me," he said, "if I make all this disappear? If I hurl you back into your bed in the Mission Inn? Or should I set you down on the leafy street in New Orleans where your lady friend lives?"

I felt the blood rise in my face.

"Get away from me," I said. "If you are what you say you are, then you know no harm can come from me going back to Vitale. From my helping another human being in dire need."

"The hell with Vitale!" he snarled. "The hell with him and his filthy entanglements. I will not let you be lost."

His fingers were digging into my flesh and it was plainly painful. The sound of the crowd and the music had become louder and louder and now it seemed deafening to me, just as the lights had become a kind of engulfing glare.

I was struggling with all my senses to know the moment, to know my thoughts, to know what to do.

A great riot of applause and shouts from the crowd shocked me. And at this moment, he locked his arm around me and started to drag me across the floor.

I drew back. "Get thee behind me, Satan!" I whispered. And I drew back my fist, and then struck him with one fine blow to the face that sent him flying backwards away from me, as if he were made of nothing but air.

I saw his form rushing away, as if down a huge tunnel of light. Indeed the very fabric of the world around me was ripped, and his body exploded in that rip into huge splashes of blinding fire. I shut my eyes. I couldn't help it. I fell down on my knees. The light was volcanic and searing. A huge cry filled my ears that became a kind of howl.

A voice spoke, "Tell me your name!"

I tried to see but the light still blinded me. I covered my face with my hands, trying to peer through my fingers, but all I could see was this rolling fire.

"Tell me your name!" came the voice again, and I heard the answer, like a hiss, "Ankanoc! Let me go."

The voice spoke again, in unmistakable denunciation, though I couldn't hear the words. *Ankanoc, go back to Hell.* He'd been banished, and the force that had sent him fleeing was still near.

There was a rolling roar, which grew louder and louder, and even though my eyes were closed, I knew the light was gone. *Ankanoc.* It was reverberating in my mind and I had the sense I would never forget it. I thought I knew the voice that had demanded this name, that had demanded that the being leave, and it was Malchiah's voice, but I wasn't sure. I was shaken to the bone.

I opened my eyes.

I found myself kneeling on the flags. The crowd was close around me, same laughter, voices and dim soaring musical notes. My head throbbed. My shoulders hurt.

Malchiah was kneeling next to me, supporting me, but he wasn't really visible to me. I felt his hands steadying me. In a soundless voice, he said, "Now you know his name. Call him by name, in whatever guise he comes to you, and he must answer! Remember this, for now and for later and for always. Ankanoc. Now I leave you to do what you must do."

Lies, belief system, beings, feeding . . .

"Don't leave me!" I whispered.

But he was gone.

A man stood beside me, a sweet, round-faced man in a long flowing red robe. I saw his hand reaching down for me as he said, "Here, let me help you up, young man, come on, it's only just past midnight, and that is far too early for you to be stumbling about." Other hands helped me to my feet.

Then, patting me on the shoulder, the man smiled and went on with his companions into the banquet room.

I was before the open doors of the palazzo. And I could see it was raining outside.

I tried to clear my head. I tried to think on all that had happened.

Just past midnight. I'd been gone that long.

What had I been thinking to let this happen, and what did I think had happened? The fear took hold of me again, the fear gradually accumulating until I couldn't think or feel. Had Malchiah really come? Had he driven the demon away? Ankanoc. Suddenly all I could visualize was his pleasing face, his seemingly solicitous manner, his undoubted charm.

I realized I was standing in the rain. I hated the rain. I didn't want to be wet. I didn't want the lute to get wet. I stood in the darkness, and the rain was pelting me and I was cold.

I closed my eyes and I prayed, to God in whom I believed, to the God of my belief system, I thought bitterly, asking Him to help me now.

I believe in You. I believe that You are here, whether I can feel it or not, or ever know for certain that it is true. I believe in the universe that You made, constructed out of Your love, and Your power. I believe that You see and know all things.

I thought silently, I believe in Your world, in Your justice, in Your coherence. I believe in what I heard in the music only moments ago. I believe in all that I can't deny. And there is the fire of love at the center of it. Let me be consumed heart and mind in this fire.

Dimly, I was aware of making a choice, but it was the only choice I could make.

My head cleared.

I heard that melody from within the palazzo, the one I'd heard when the musicians had first begun to play. I didn't know whether I was shaping it out of the distant raw threads of the music, or whether they were really playing it, so faint was the song. But I knew the melody and I began to hum it to myself. I wanted to cry.

I didn't cry. I stood there until I was calm again and resolute and the darkness did not seem to be a fatal gloom enveloping the entire world. Oh, if only Malchiah would come back, I thought, if only he would speak to me some more. Why had he let that demon come to me, that evil dybbuk? Why had he allowed it? But then who was I to ask such a question of him? I didn't set the rules for this world. I didn't set the rules for this mission.

I had to return to Vitale now.

Malchiah was giving me the opportunity to do this, to fulfill the mission, and that is exactly what I meant to do.

I saw, far to my left, the alleyway through which I'd come to this place, and I hurried towards it, and then down the long alley towards the piazza before Vitale's house.

I was running with my head down when, just before the gate of the house, Pico caught me and threw a mantle over my head and shoulders. He brought me inside the gateway, out of the rain, and quickly dried my face with a clean dry cloth.

A lone torch blazed in its iron sconce, and on a small table was a simple iron candelabrum with three burning candles.

I stood shivering, hating the cold. It was only a little warmer here, but gradually the sharpness of the chill was going away.

In my mind, I saw the face of Ankanoc and I heard his words again, "a belief system," and I heard the long sentences he'd spoken and all the familiar phrases that had spilled from his lips. I saw the passion in his eyes. Then I heard that hiss when he'd confessed his name.

I saw the fire again and heard the deafening roar that came with it. I rested my weight against the damp stone wall.

A growing awareness came to me: you never know anything for certain, even when your faith is great. You don't know it. Your longing, your anguish, can be without end. Even here, in this strange house in another century, with all the proofs of Heaven given to me, I didn't really know all that I longed to know. I couldn't escape fear. Only a moment ago an angel had spoken to me, but now I was alone. And the longing to know was pain, because it was a longing for all tension and misery to end. And they do not really ever end.

"My master says for you to leave," said Pico desperately. "Here I have money for you from him. He thanks you."

"I don't need money."

He seemed glad of that and put away the purse.

"But Master," he said, "I beg you. Do not go. My master is locked up now in Signore Antonio's house. Fr. Piero has demanded that he be locked up until more priests come. They are holding him on account of the demon."

"I won't abandon him," I said.

"Thank Heaven," said Pico, and he started to weep. "Thank

Heaven." He said it over and over. "If my master is tried for witchcraft the verdict will be certain. He will die."

"I will do my best to see this never happens!"

I turned to go into the house.

"No, Master, please, don't go in. The demon has been quiet only a few hours. If we go towards the stairs, he will know it and start again."

"Stay here then, but I'm going to talk to this demon," I said. I picked up the iron candelabrum. "I've just been talking to another one, and this demon holds no new fear for me."

CHAPTER TEN

As soon as I reached the stone stairs, I heard the dybbuk. He was high above me. I thought of Vitale's words to me that "upstairs" he had found the synagogue of the house, with its sacred books. I went on upward, shielding the shivering flames of the candles, past the doors of Vitale's study and towards the top story of the house.

The noises grew louder and more insistent. Something shattered. There were thumps and knocks, as objects perhaps struck the walls.

Finally I found myself in the open doorway to a large room. Silence. Its ceiling was somewhat lower than those below, but not by much.

At once the light revealed the distant gleaming silver doors of the Ark or repository which no doubt held the sacred books of Moses. This was set into the eastern wall. To one side, a podium of sorts faced the room, with several dusty benches before it, and further to the right there stood a large painted and gilded screen. Behind this was a long bench, once intended in all probability for the women who might attend the service or sermon here. The walls were paneled in dark wood, very rich, but not so dark that I couldn't see the many inscriptions on them, painted in black Hebrew letters. A table lay to one side of the podium on which there was a heap of scrolls.

Fine silver chandeliers hung from the ceiling. The windows were shuttered and bolted. And my candelabrum was of course the only light.

Suddenly the benches before me started to vibrate, then to move, one bench slamming into another, and the chandeliers began to creak on their silver chains.

A small bound book was lifted from one of the benches and this came flying at me, so that I had to duck. It landed behind me on the floor.

"Who are you?" I demanded. "If you're a dybbuk, I demand that you tell me your name!"

All the benches were moving, crashing into one another, and the painted screen came down with a huge clatter. Again objects were being hurled at me, and I had to get out of the doorway, shielding myself instinctively with my right hand. There was a hollow sound, a rumble, rather like the noise I'd heard when Ankanoc had been banished, but this seemed made by a human voice. It was so loud I covered my ears.

"In the name of God," I said, "I demand that you tell me your name." But this only increased the creature's fury. One of the chandeliers began to rock furiously back and forth until it was ripped from its chains, and thundered into the benches below.

I slumped down on the floor, as if I was cowering, but I was not. I watched another chandelier come crashing down on the benches, and tried not to blink or shudder at the sheer noise.

Putting the candelabrum on the floor, I sat very still. If this thing blew out the lights, I would be very uncomfortable, but so far it had not done that, and as I remained there without moving or speaking, it grew quiet again.

Slowly, I reached back for my lute and brought it around

into my lap. I wasn't sure what I meant to do, but I tightened the strings of the lute, plucking it very softly, to tune it. Closing my eyes, I began to play from memory that melody that I'd heard in the Cardinal's palace. I thought, without words, of what that music had meant to me when I'd been arguing with Ankanoc. I thought of the coherence, the eloquence of it, the way it spoke to me of a world in which harmony was infinitely more than dream, in which beauty pointed to the divine. I was almost weeping suddenly as I gave in to the music, trusting myself to reconstruct the melody and make it my own with any changes that memory couldn't support.

The soft notes of the lute echoed off the walls. I grew a little bolder, playing faster, and with greater variation, and slowly taking the melody into a melancholy comment on itself. I began to hum with the lower notes, and then to sing under my breath in low monosyllables, na nah, na nah nah, na, letting my fingers and my voice take me where they would. The tears came to my eyes. I let them spill down my face. I began to sing under my breath the words of a psalm.

" 'Oh, Lord of my salvation, when I cry out in the darkness before you, let my prayers reach you.' " I struggled, unable to remember, paraphrasing, " 'I am near to the brink of Sheol. Bend your ear to my pain.' "

I went on singing, breaking into words when phrases came back to me, humming if no words came. My eyes moved over the shadowy room before me, and I realized that I was not alone.

There standing before the repository, and not very far away from me, was a small elderly man.

We looked at one another, and his face revealed a great astonishment, and it wasn't difficult to figure why. *He was amazed that I could see him, just as I was myself.*

I had stopped playing. I merely looked at him, determined

to show no fear, and indeed I felt no fear. I felt only a growing excitement and a wonder, and a desperation to know what to do.

"You are no dybbuk," I whispered under my breath. He didn't appear to hear the words. He was looking me over in detail. And I did the same now with him, memorizing all that I saw with the old training of an assassin, determined to miss nothing of what was being presented to me here.

He was smallish, a little bent and very ancient, with a bald pate and a rich mane of long white hair falling down to his shoulders. He had a white mustache and a white beard. His black velvet clothes, though once elegant, were now shabby and dusty and torn here and there. Blue tassels were sewn to the ends of his mantle and he wore the hated yellow badge over his heart, which marked him as a Jew. He stood collected, fiercely examining me through a pair of glittering spectacles, with small burning eyes.

Spectacles. I hadn't known people in this era had such things. But he was definitely wearing spectacles and now and then the flames of my candles glittered in the lenses.

Malchiah, give me the grace to speak to him.

"You realize that I can see you," I said. "I don't come as an enemy. I come only to discover why it is that you haunt. What has left you so restless? What has left you unwilling to go on into the light?"

For a second he was silent, motionless and reflective. Then he started towards me.

I thought my heart would stop. He came on steadily until he stood directly in front of me. I held my breath. He was seemingly solid, human, breathing, as he looked at me from beneath his white brows.

It was no consolation to me that I myself was a spirit in this realm, that he was no more of a miracle than I was myself. I was afraid, but determined to conceal it.

He walked past me and out into the passage.

At once I had the candelabrum, and forgetting the lute, I turned and went behind him. He went on towards the staircase and then began a rapid soundless descent.

I followed.

Not once did he look back. Hunched and small he moved rapidly, with the dexterity of a ghost perhaps, until he came to the bolted cellar door. He passed through this, and I hurriedly unbolted it to follow him, discovering him near the bottom of the stairs as I rushed after him, the candles slowly revealing the wreckage of the cellar all around us.

Broken tables and chairs lay everywhere on the flags. Dusty wine casks lined the walls. Bundles of old furniture, tied with rope, were stacked above the casks, with some broken open and spilling their shattered contents down to the floor. Hundreds of moldering books lay in heaps with spines broken and pages crushed.

Lamp stands and candelabra had been overthrown, and baskets scattered. Old garments had been twisted and strewn about.

The small elderly man now stood in the middle of the floor staring at me.

"What is it you want me to know?" I asked. I wanted to make the Sign of the Cross, but this would be an affront to him. "In the name of the Lord in Heaven, what is it that I can do?"

He went into a rage.

He bellowed and roared at me, stamping his foot over and over against the cellar floor, and glaring down at it, and then he began to reach for those small things that already lay strewn about. He grabbed hold of a bottle and smashed it on the stones. He hurled books at the stones. He tore loose parchment pages and attempted vainly to fling them down, furious as they floated and swirled around him. He stamped and pointed, and bellowed as if he were a wild beast.

"Stop this, please, I beg you!" I cried out. "You are no dybbuk. I know this. I hear your cries. Tell me your heart."

But I couldn't tell whether or not he heard this over his own cries.

He began to hurl objects at me. Chair legs, bits of crockery, broken bottles—whatever he could snatch up, he threw at me.

It seemed the whole cellar was shaking; bundles of furniture were tumbling down off the kegs as if we were in an earthquake. A bottle of wine struck me hard on the side of my head and I felt the vinegary liquid pour down over my shoulder. I backed up, reeling, dizzy. But I held the lighted candelabrum firmly as if for my life.

I was tempted to condemn him for this and argue with him, to appeal to his gratitude that I had deigned to come here on his account, but I realized immediately that this was boastful and proud and stupid. He was miserable. What were my intentions to him?

I bowed my head and prayed softly. *Lord, please do not let me fail as I did with Lodovico.* Again, I chose a half-remembered psalm, and as I chanted the ancient words of appeal, he gradually stopped.

He stood still pointing to the floor. Yes, he was pointing.

Suddenly I heard Pico in the doorway at the top of the stairs.

"Master, for the love of Heaven, come out!" he cried.

No, not now, I thought desperately.

The ghost had vanished.

Every portable object in the room seemed suddenly to be flying through the air. The candles were blown out.

In hopeless darkness, I dropped the candelabrum, turned and ran towards the dim light at the top of the steps. I was certain I could feel hands pulling at me, fingers snatching at my hair, breath against my face.

In sheer panic, I kept going until I could grab ahold of Pico, and push him out of the way, and slam the cellar door. I threw the bolt.

I lay back catching my breath.

"Master, there's blood on your face," Pico cried.

From behind the door came the most piteous howling and then a thunderous noise as if the large wine casks were being rolled across the cellar floor.

"Never mind the blood," I said. "Take me to Signore Antonio. I have to speak to him now."

I headed out of the house.

"At this hour?" Pico protested, but I wouldn't be deterred.

"He knows who this ghost is, he must know," I said. I tried to remember what I'd been told. A Hebrew scholar had lived in the house, yes, twenty years ago. This Hebrew scholar had arranged the synagogue on the top floor. Had Signore Antonio never guessed that this man might be the ghost?

We pounded on the doors of Signore Antonio's house until the night watchman appeared and, seeing who we were, sleepily let us in.

"I must see the master immediately," I told the old man, but he only shook his head as if he were deaf. It was amazing, I thought, how many elderly and infirm servants this house included. It was Pico who took up a single candle and led the way upstairs.

Signore Antonio's bedchamber was filled with lighted

lamps. The doors were wide open and I could see him plainly, kneeling in his long wool robe on the bare floor at the foot of his bed. His head was bare and sweating in the light, and his hands were outstretched in the form of a cross. Surely he was praying for his son.

He started when I appeared in the door. And then stared at me with muted outrage.

"Why have you come here now?" he demanded. "I thought you'd fled for your life."

"I've seen the ghost who haunts the other house," I said. "I've seen him plainly and surely you know who he is."

I came into the room, and offered my hands to help him to his feet. This he accepted, as it was very difficult for him at his age, and then he backed up and, turning, found his way to one of his many enormous heavily carved chairs. He sank down on the cushions and, rubbing his nose for a moment as though he was in pain, he looked up at me.

"I don't believe in ghosts!" he said. "Dybbuks, yes, demons, yes, but ghosts, no."

"Well, think again on it. This ghost is a small elderly man. He wears a black velvet tunic, long, like that of a scholar, but he has blue tassels sewn on the edges of his mantle. He wears the yellow 'badge of shame' on his tunic, and peers at the world through spectacles." I made the gesture to describe them with my fingers before my eyes. "He has a bald head and long gray hair and beard."

He was speechless.

"Is this the Hebrew scholar who lived in this house twenty years ago?" I asked. "Do you know this man's name?"

He didn't answer but he was mightily impressed by what I'd described. He stared off, stunned and seemingly miserable.

"For the sake of Heaven, man, tell me if you know who this

man is," I said. "Vitale is locked up under your roof. He'll be tried by the Inquisition for having a—."

"Yes, yes, I've been trying to stop all this," he cried, raising his hand. He drew in his breath and, after a moment of silence, he seemed to surrender himself, with a long sigh, to what had to be done. "Yes, I know who this ghost is."

"Do you know why he haunts? Do you know what he wants?"

He shook his head. Clearly all this was excruciating for him.

"The cellar, what has it to do with the cellar? He led me to the cellar. He pointed to the stone floor."

He let out a long agonizing groan. He put his hands to his face, then stared forward over his own fingers.

"You really saw this?" he whispered.

"Yes. I saw this. He rages, he bellows, he cries in pain. And he points to the floor."

"Oh, no, don't say any more," he pleaded. "Why was I fool enough to think it could not be?" He turned away from me, as if he couldn't bear my scrutiny, or anyone's for that matter, and he bowed his head.

"Can you not tell everyone what you know?" I asked. "Can you not testify that this thing has nothing to do with Vitale, or poor Lodovico, or Niccolò? Signore Antonio, you must tell what you know."

"Pull the bell rope," he said.

I did as he asked.

When his servant appeared, another ancient relic of a human being, he told the old man that at dawn he was to gather the entire household to the nearby house where the ghost raged. This gathering must include Fr. Piero, Niccolò and Vitale and that all were to be assembled around the table in the dining hall, which should be dusted and provided with lamps and chairs. Bread, fruit, wine, all should be furnished, as he had a story to tell.

I took my leave of him.

Pico, who'd been hovering in the passage, took me to Vitale's door. When I called Vitale's name he answered, in a low dispirited voice. I told him not to be afraid. I had seen the ghost and its mystery would soon be explained.

Then I allowed myself to be led to a small bedchamber with painted walls, and curious as I was as to everything about it, I sank down on the coffered bed and went fast asleep.

I awoke with first morning light. I'd been dreaming of Ankanoc. We'd been sitting together, talking in some comfortable place, and he had said, with all his seeming charm, "Didn't I tell you? There are millions of souls lost in systems of pain and grief and meaningless attachment. There is no justice, no mercy, no God. There is no witness to what we suffer, except our own." *Spirits using you, feeding off your emotions, no god, no devil . . .*

Quietly in the small bedchamber, I answered him, or I answered myself. "There is mercy," I whispered. "And there is justice, and there is One who witnesses everything. And above all, there is love."

CHAPTER ELEVEN

THE FAMILY WAS GATHERED IN THE DINING ROOM OF the unfortunate house when I arrived. The ghost was rampaging in the cellar and now and then sending great howls and roars through all the rooms.

I saw at once that there were four armed guards in attendance on Signore Antonio, hovering about his chair at the head of the table. He looked rested and resolved, and solemn in his black velvet, head bowed, and hands pressed together as if in prayer.

Niccolò looked marvelously improved, and this was the first time I'd seen him in regular clothes, if the clothes of this time could ever be called regular. He was clad in black like his father, and so was Vitale, who sat beside him, and looked up at me with timid eyes.

Fr. Piero was seated at the foot of the table, and beside him on his right were two other clerics, and someone with a stack of papers and an inkwell and quill pen who looked, of course, like a clerk. Abundant food lay on the immense carved sideboard, and a collection of frightened servants, including Pico, cleaved to the walls.

"Sit there," said Signore Antonio, pointing me to his right. I obeyed.

"I say again I am opposed to this!" said Fr. Piero, "this communing with spirits or whatever it is reasoned to be! This house must be exorcised now. I am prepared to begin."

"Enough of all that," said Signore Antonio. "I know now who haunts this house and I will tell you who he is and why he haunts. And I charge you, not a word of this is ever to leave this chamber."

Reluctantly the priests agreed, but I could see that they did not see themselves as being bound by this. Possibly it would not matter.

The noises from the cellar continued, and once again, I was convinced that the ghost was rolling the heavy casks of wine over the floor.

At Signore Antonio's gesture the guards closed the door of the dining room, and we had a measure of quiet in which Signore Antonio began to speak.

"LET ME BEGIN MANY YEARS AGO, WHEN I WAS A young student in Florence and had enjoyed myself to some considerable extent at the Court of the Medici, and was not at all glad to see the fierce Savonarola come into that city. Do you know who this is?"

"Tell us, Father," said Niccolò. "We've heard his name all our lives, but don't really know what happened at the time."

"Well, I had many friends among the Jews in Florence then as I have now, and I had scholarly friends, and one very grave teacher in particular, who was helping me to translate medical texts from Arabic which he as a great teacher of Hebrew knew very well. This man I venerated much as you boys have come to venerate your Hebrew teachers at Padua and at Montpellier. His name was Giovanni and I was deeply in his debt for the work he did for me, and sometimes felt that I did not pay him enough, for every time he gave me a beautifully prepared manuscript, I took it at once to the printer's and the book went into circulation for all my friends to see and enjoy. I would say that Giovanni's translations and annotations for me were circulated throughout Italy, as he worked very hastily and in fair copy most of the time without the slightest mistake.

"Well, Giovanni, who was my good friend and my drinking companion, depended upon me for protection when the friars would come and preach their sermons working up the populace against the Jews. So did his beloved and only son, Lionello, who was as good a friend and companion to me as I have ever had. I loved Lionello and I loved his father with all my heart.

"Now you know every Holy Week in our cities, it is the same. The doors are shut on all the Jews from Holy Thursday through Easter Sunday, as much for their protection as for anything else. And as the sermons are preached in which they are castigated as the slayers of Christ, the young ruffians make for the streets and hurl stones at any Jewish house they can find. The Jews remain indoors, safe from this onslaught, and seldom is more than a window or two broken, and when Easter Sunday is over and the crowd is quiet once more and people have gone back to their business, the Jews come out, repair the glass and all is forgotten."

"We all know this, and we know they deserve what they get," said Fr. Piero, "as they are indeed the murderers of Our Blessed Lord."

"Ah, let's not try the Jews here on fresh charges," said Signore Antonio. "Surely Vitale here is respected by the Pope's physicians and he has many members of his family in the employ of rich Romans who are glad to have him in their service."

"Will you tell us please what Holy Week has to do with the ravings of this spirit?" Fr. Piero shot back. "Is he some Jewish ghost who imagines himself wrongly accused of the murder of Christ?"

Signore Antonio glared at the priest scornfully. And quite suddenly there came a racket from the cellar like none that had been heard before.

Signore Antonio's face was very grave. And he stared at Fr. Piero as though he despised him, but he didn't answer right away. Fr. Piero was shaken and enraged by the noise. So were the other priests who were with him. In fact, everybody was shaken, even me. Vitale sat flinching at every new assault from the cellar. And doors throughout the house began to slam as if in a powerful draft.

Raising his voice above the sounds, Signore Antonio spoke again:

"A terrible thing befell my friend Giovanni in Florence," he said. "A thing that involved Lionello whom I so loved." His face grew pale, and he turned to the side for a moment as though averting his eyes from the very memory he was about to report. "I only now as a father who has lost a son can begin to grasp what this meant for Giovanni," he said. "At the time I felt too keenly my own pain. But what befell Giovanni's only son was more miserable than anything even that has happened to my Lodovico under my roof."

He swallowed, and in a strained voice went on.

"You must remember these were days unlike the days we now enjoy in Rome," he said, "where the Holy Father keeps a check on the friars that they won't work the populace into a frenzy against the Jews."

"It's never the friars' intention to do these things," said Fr. Piero. His voice was as patient and gentle as he could manage it. "When they preach in Holy Week they mean only to remind us all of our sins. We are all the slayers of Our Blessed Lord. We are all responsible for His Death on the Cross. And as you said yourself, it is no more than a drama, this throwing of stones at the houses of the Jews, and everyone returns to normal intercourse within a matter of days."

"Ah, listen to me. In Florence in that last year that I lived there, during such a happy time with my friends at the court of the great Lorenzo, a dreadful accusation was made during Holy Week against Giovanni's beloved son, Lionello, and it was an accusation that could not have contained a particle of truth.

"Savonarola had begun his preaching, he had begun insisting that the populace cleanse itself of sin. He had begun recommending the burning of all items that had to do with licentious living. And there was at his behest a group of young men, toughs all, who went about attempting to enforce his will. It was always this way with the friars. They had what were commonly called the friar's boys."

"Nobody approves of such things," said Fr. Piero.

"Yet they congregate," said Signore Antonio. "And a mob of them brought their fantastic charges against Lionello, accusing him of profaning the images of the Blessed Virgin publicly and in three different spots. As if a Jew would have been mad enough to do such a thing once. And here they put a triple charge against him. And at the behest of the friars and their ravings, a triple punishment for the young man was decreed.

"Now, mark my word, the young man was innocent. I knew Lionello! I loved him, as I've told you. What would have driven a man of intellect and polish, of love of poetry and music, to mock the Madonna and before others in three different places? And to show you how very preposterous all this is, imagine that he had committed some blasphemous act in one spot. Would he have been allowed to seek out a second and a third for the same crime?

"But these were mad times in Florence. Savonarola was gaining power. The Medici were losing their grip.

"And so this sentence was decreed on the luckless Lionello, whom I knew, you understand, knew and loved as I did Giovanni, my teacher, knew and loved as I do my son's friend Vitale, who sits with us here."

He paused as if he had no taste to go on. No one spoke. And only then did I realize that the ghost was quiet. The ghost was not making a sound.

I didn't know whether anyone else realized it, because we were all looking at Signore Antonio.

"What was this sentence?" asked Fr. Piero.

The silence continued. Nowhere in the building did anything rattle or shatter, or break.

I wasn't going to draw anyone's attention to this. I listened instead.

"It was decreed," said Signore Antonio, "that Lionello should be taken first to the corner of the hospital of Santa Maria Nuova, at San Nofri, to an image he had supposedly defaced, and there have his hand chopped off, which in fact took place."

Vitale's face was rigid but his lips were white. Niccolò was plainly horrified.

"From there," said Signore Antonio, "the young man was dragged by the mob to a painted Pietà at Santa Maria in Campo, where his remaining hand was chopped off. And then it was the intention of the populace to drag him to the third scene of his supposed transgressions, the Madonna at Or San Michele, and there to have his eyes put out. But the mob, some two thousand strong by this time, did not wait for this last act of abomination to be committed on the hapless youth, but grabbed him from those accompanying him and mutilated him on the spot."

The two priests were downcast. Fr. Piero shook his head.

"May the Lord have mercy on his soul," he said. "The mobs of Florence are altogether worse than the mobs of Rome."

"Are they?" asked Signore Antonio. "The young man, with stumps for hands, his eyes torn out, his body mutilated, clung to life for a few days. And in my house!"

Niccolò lowered his eyes and shook his head.

"And I knelt beside him with his weeping father," said Signore Antonio, "and it was after that, after the beautiful young man who had been Lionello was laid to rest, that I insisted Giovanni come to Rome with me.

"Savonarola appeared unstoppable. The Jews would soon be driven from Florence altogether. And I had my abundant property here, and my connections at the court of the Pope who would never stand for such barbarity in the Holy City, or so we hoped and prayed. So my Maestro Giovanni, shaken, shocked, barely able to speak or think or take a taste of water, came with me for safe refuge here."

"And it was to this man," asked Fr. Piero, "that you gave this house?"

"Yes, it was to this man that I gave the library I had accumulated, a study in which to work, luxuries which I hoped would comfort him, and the promise of students who would come to him to seek his wisdom as soon as his spirit could be healed. Elders from the Jewish community came to set up the synagogue on the top floor of this house, and to gather in prayer there with Giovanni who was too crushed in spirit to go out the front door into the streets.

"But how, I ask you, can a father who has seen such barbarity done to his son ever be healed?"

Signore Antonio looked at the priests. He looked at Vitale, and at me. He looked at his son, Niccolò.

"And remember my wounded soul," he whispered. "For I

had loved young Lionello myself very much. He was the companion of my heart, Niccolò, as Vitale has always been to you. He had been my tutor when my teacher didn't have patience for me. He had been the one to write verses with me back and forth across the tavern table. He had been the one to play the lute as you do, Toby, and I had seen his hands chopped off, thrown to dogs as if they were garbage, and his body torn all but to pieces before his eyes were finally put out."

"Better that he died, the poor soul," said Fr. Piero. "May God forgive those who did these things to him."

"Yes, may God forgive them. I do not know if Giovanni could forgive them, or whether I could forgive them.

"But Giovanni lived in this house like a ghost. And not a ghost who hurls bottles against walls or rattles doors, or heaves ink pots into the air or throws things against a cellar floor. He lived as if he had no heart left. As if he had nothing in him, while I, day and night, talked of better times, of better things, of his marrying again, as he had lost his wife so many years ago, of his perhaps having another son."

He stopped and shook his head. "Perhaps this was the wrong thing to suggest to him. Perhaps it wounded him more deeply than I supposed. All I know is that he kept his few precious articles to himself, his books to himself, and would never settle into the library or make himself at home with me at any repast. At last I gave up the idea of making him live in and enjoy this house as its proper occupant, and I went on back to my own, and came to see him as often as I could only to find him, often as not, in the cellar of all places, and reluctant to come up to me unless he was certain I was alone. The servants told me he had hidden his treasure in the cellar, and some of his most precious books.

"He was in essence a destroyed man. The scholar no longer

existed in him. Memory was too painful for him. The present didn't exist.

"Then came Holy Week as it does each year and those who were Jews in these streets shut up their doors as always and stayed within as the law requires. And the roughs of the neighborhood, the lowborn, the foolish, went about as always after the heated Lenten sermons heaving rocks at the houses of the Jews and cursing them for the killing of Our Lord Jesus Christ.

"I thought nothing of it as regards Giovanni because he was in one of my houses and I never expected the slightest harm would come to him, but on Good Friday night, I was called by my servants to go at once. The mob had attacked the house, and Giovanni had gone out to face them, weeping, howling in rage, hurling rocks at them as they hurled rocks at him.

"My guards struggled to put an end to the melee. I dragged Giovanni back inside.

"But Giovanni's desperate actions had touched off a riot. Hundreds were pounding on the doors and the walls, threatening to tear the place apart.

"Now there are many hiding places in this house, behind paneled walls, off staircases which one might not discover for years. But the most secure place is in the cellar, beneath the stones in the middle of the floor.

"With all my strength, I dragged Giovanni down there. 'You must hide,' I told him, 'until I can make this mob go away.'

"He was bloodied and bleeding, cut badly about the head and face. I don't think he understood me. I lifted the false flags that conceal an underground storage space, and I forced him down into it, roughly and desperately, insisting he remain there until the danger was past. I don't think he understood what was happening. He fought me madly. Finally I struck him a blow that made him go quiet. Like a child, he turned on his side and, pulling up his knees, put a hand over his face.

"It was then that I glimpsed his treasure and his books in this hiding place, and I thought, it is good these things are hidden, for the ruffians outside are about to breach the house.

"He was shaking and moaning as I put the stones back into place.

"The windows of the house were being broken, the door was being rammed again and again.

"Finally, surrounded by the servants, and armed as best I could be, I opened the door and told the mob that the Jew they sought was not here. I let the ringleaders in to see for themselves.

"I threatened them all with fierce retaliation if they dared harm one item of my property. And my guards and servants watched them as they roamed about the main rooms, down into the cellar and up through some of the bedchambers before finally leaving a good deal more quietly than they had come in. None of them had bothered with the top floor. They did not see the synagogue or the sacred books. What they wanted was blood. They wanted the Jew who had fought them and struck them, and that one they could not find.

"Once the house was secured again, I went to the cellar. I lifted the stones, eager to free my poor friend, and attend to him, and what do you think I found?"

"He was dead," said Fr. Piero in a low voice.

Signore Antonio nodded. Then he looked off again as if he wished, for all the world, to be absolutely alone now rather than telling this tale.

"Did I kill him?" he asked. "Or did he die from the blows he'd received from the others? How could I know? I knew only he was dead. His suffering was ended. And for the moment, I merely moved the stones back into place.

"That night another mob came, and the house was once again the target for their abuse. But I had left it locked and secured, and when the toughs saw that no lights burned within, they finally went away.

"Soldiers came on Monday after Easter. Was it true, a Jew known to me had attacked Christians in Holy Week when it was forbidden that a Jew be seen in the streets?

"I gave the usual noncommittal responses. How was I to know such a thing? 'There is no Jew here anymore. Search the house if you like.' And search the house they did. 'He's gone, fled,' I insisted. They left soon enough. But more than once they came back with the same questions.

"I was miserable with grief and guilt. The more I brooded on it, the more I cursed myself for my roughness with Giovanni, that I had dragged him to the cellar, that I had beaten him to make him lie quiet. I could not bear what I had done, and I could not bear the pain I felt in remembering all that had gone before. And somehow in my misery, I dared to blame him. I dared to blame him that I had not been able to protect him, and heal him. I dared to curse him for the sheer misery that I had felt."

Again, he stopped and looked away. A long moment passed.

"You left him there, buried in the cellar," said Fr. Piero.

Signore Antonio nodded, slowly turning to face the priest again.

"Of course I told myself that I would soon attend to his burial. I would wait until no one even remembered the riot of Holy Week and I would go to the elders of his community and tell them that he must be laid to rest."

"But you never did it," said Fr. Piero softly.

"No," said Signore Antonio. "I never did it. I shut up the house and abandoned it. Now and then I stored things there, old furniture, books, wine, whatever had to be moved from this house. But I never entered the house myself. This is the first time, the very first time since, that I have entered the house."

When it was clear that he had paused again, I said softly, "The ghost has gone quiet. The ghost went quiet when you began to speak."

Signore Antonio bowed his head and put his hand to his eyes. I thought he would break into sobs, but he only took a ragged breath, and then went on,

"I always thought," he said, "that I would tend to this, someday, I would have the proper prayers said for him by his own. But I never did.

"Before the end of the year I was married, I began to travel. My wife and I buried more than one child over the years, but my beloved son, Niccolò, whom you see here, has cheated death more than once. Aye, more than once. And there was always some reason not to approach the abandoned house, not to disturb the dust of the cellar floor, not to face the questions of the Jews as to their old friend and scholar Giovanni, not to explain why I had done what I did."

"But you didn't murder him," Fr. Piero said. "It was not your doing."

"No," said Signore Antonio, "but he was murdered nevertheless."

The priest sighed and nodded.

Signore Antonio looked pointedly at Vitale.

"When I met you, I loved you immediately," he said. "You can't imagine what a pleasure it was to bring you into the old house, to show you the synagogue and the library, and to put before you so many of Giovanni's books."

Vitale nodded gravely. There were tears in his eyes.

Signore Antonio went quiet. Then spoke again. "I wondered if my old friend would be pleased that you were living under the old roof, if he would be pleased that you were going through his many books. And I even wondered more than once if I might ask you to pray for the soul of that scholar who had lived in the house before."

"I will pray for him," Vitale whispered.

Signore Antonio looked directly at Fr. Piero.

"Do you still insist it is a demon raging here, a Jewish dybbuk? Or don't you see now that it was the ghost of my old friend whose memory I consigned to oblivion because I could not bear his pain or my own?"

The priest did not answer.

Signore Antonio looked at me. I could see that he wanted to tell them of my description of the ghost I'd seen, but he did not. He did not want to indict me for seeing spirits or talking to them. I said nothing.

"Why did I not consider the truth of this in the beginning?" he asked, looking once again at Fr. Piero. "And who now is charged, justly, with seeing to it that my old friend's remains are at last properly laid to rest?"

We sat in quiet for a long time. Fr. Piero made the Sign of the Cross and murmured a prayer.

Finally Signore Antonio rose to his feet and we all rose with him. "Bring light," he said to the servants, and we followed him now out of the dining room and down to the main floor.

There he took a candelabrum from Pico, and unbolting the door to the cellar, he led the way down the stairs.

The scene was far worse than it had been only hours ago when I had come to seek the ghost. Every bit of furniture had been broken into pieces both large and small. Every book in sight had been ripped apart. Several of the casks, apparently empty, had been staved in, and broken glass glittered all over the flags.

But there was no unusual sound here. In fact, there was no sound at all except for our own respiration, and the soft steps of

Signore Antonio as he approached the very spot where I had seen the ghost take a stand.

Signore Antonio gave the order for the floor to be cleared. At once his servants and guards swept back the debris. Their very boots at once marked the few hollow flags in the floor.

Quickly, with prying fingers, the stones were turned up and over and free of the space beneath them.

And there, in the light of the candelabrum, for all to see, was the small skeleton of the man, a loose chain of bones held together by the rotting remnants of his clothes.

All around him in bundles lay his books. And beside his books his sacks of treasure. But he himself, how he might have suffered in this tiny place, weeping, wounded, untended. The bones made it plain, to the bones of the hand that reached up to clutch the bundle that cradled his head, and the bones that tried to hold forever the precious book beside him.

How small and fragile lay the skull. And how in the light the little spectacles glittered.

CHAPTER TWELVE

THAT AFTERNOON, THE JEWISH ELDERS WERE INVITED to the house. Signore Antonio met with them in private, leaving Niccolò and Vitale and me to ourselves.

A coffin was brought that evening for the remains of Giovanni, and we accompanied the Jewish elders by torchlight on the long trek to the Jewish Cemetery where the remains were laid to rest. All prayers were said as they were meant to be said.

No ruffians were allowed to harry the funeral procession. And it was late when we returned to the quiet house. It was as if the ghost had never been there. The servants were still sweeping the passages and stairways, in spite of the hour, and candles burned in many rooms.

Signore Antonio summoned Vitale to join him in the library, and there told him, as Vitale would tell me later, that Giovanni's wealth had been divided with one half being given to the Jewish elders, and the other bequeathed to Vitale who would not only pray for the soul of Giovanni, and commemorate his death in every acceptable way, but would begin the collection and restoration of Giovanni's many literary works. Signore Antonio had copies of many of these books, and Vitale would hunt down those that had been lost. This would be

Vitale's principal task for Signore Antonio for some time to come.

Meanwhile Niccolò would move into the house as had been planned and Vitale would commence work as his secretary again.

In other words, the prayer of Vitale had been answered, and in some ways, so had the prayers he had uttered in the synagogue, in that he was now, thanks to the inheritance from Giovanni, on his way to being a rich man.

I knew my time was coming to a close. In fact, I did not know why Malchiah had not already come for me.

I visited Signore Antonio at his house just as he was heading for bed, and told him that I would soon be leaving, as my job was finished.

He gave me a long and meaningful look. I knew that he wanted to ask me how or why I'd seen Giovanni's spirit, but he didn't, as this was a dangerous subject in Rome, and he was disposed, obviously, to let it go. I wanted to tell him how sorry I was that Lodovico had taken his own life. I tried to think of the words, but I couldn't. Finally, I put out my arms and he drew me close in a firm embrace, and thanked me for all I'd done.

"You know you can remain with us for as long as you like," he said. "I am delighted to have a lutenist in my house. And I would love to hear all the songs you know. Were I not in mourning for Lodovico, I would beg for you to play something for me now. But the point is, you can remain with us. Why don't you stay?"

He was completely earnest in this, and for a moment I couldn't think of an answer. I looked at him. I thought of all that had happened in these two days, and it felt as if I'd known him for years. I felt the same pain I'd experienced in my first mission for Malchiah, when I'd become so very close to the people in England whom I'd been sent to help.

I thought about Liona and Little Toby, and of Malchiah's assurance to me that I knew how to love. If that was true, it was a recent bit of learning, and I was still a dreadful beginner at loving and would have to somehow make up for ten years of bitterness and failure to love anyone at all. Whatever the case, I loved this man now and I didn't want to go. Much as I wanted to return to Liona and Toby, I didn't want to go.

Niccolò was asleep when I came to his room, and I let my farewell be a simple kiss on his forehead. His color had returned, and he was sleeping deeply and well.

When I got back to the "other" house, I found Vitale in the library where we had first talked. He was already reading through some of Giovanni's translations, and he had a stack of books ready for further examination.

Those volumes that had been in the cellar hiding place were badly damaged from mold and damp, but he could make out well enough the titles and the subject matter, and would seek replacements far and wide. He was now completely taken with the life of Giovanni, and Giovanni's accomplishments, and he spoke of seeking out others who had been Giovanni's pupils in years past.

It turned out Pico had told him of our visit to the house in the early hours, and Pico had overheard my conversations with the ghost and my conversation with Signore Antonio in which I had described the ghost in detail. So Vitale knew it all.

He said that if it were not for me surely the Inquisition would have destroyed him, of that he was well aware.

"It was never your doing, any of it," I reminded him. He sat there shuddering, as if he could not quite get the earlier danger out of his mind.

"But my prayer, my prayer for fame and fortune, do you think it waked this spirit?"

"The opening of the house itself waked the spirit," I said. "And now the spirit is completely at peace."

When we embraced, I was close to weeping.

Near midnight, when all slept, I went up to the synagogue, retrieved the lute from the floor where I'd left it, and sat on one of the benches in the darkness wondering what I should do.

The servants had swept the place, cleared away the fallen chandeliers, and dusted things. I could see all this by a bit of light that leaked in from a torch on the nearby stairs.

I sat there wondering: Why am I still here? I had said my farewells because I'd felt an overwhelming desire to say them, a certainty that I was meant to say them, but I did not know what to do now.

Finally, I resolved to leave the house.

Only Pico was on guard at the front door. I gave him most of the gold in my pockets. He didn't want it, but I insisted.

I saved only what I thought I might need to find a warm place in a tavern where I might listen to the music and wait in the hopes that Malchiah would soon come for me, and I felt strongly that he would.

Soon, I was walking, very far away from the part of town I knew, through ink black streets where seldom a dog barked or a hooded figure hurried by. My thoughts were heavy. My failure to save Lodovico weighed on me no matter how many times I reminded myself that the Maker knew the hearts and minds of all of us, and He and He alone could judge the misery or confusion, or poison, that had led Lodovico to his dark path. More than ever I realized that what we know of another soul's salvation is essentially nothing. We are always thinking and talking about our own souls, and of our own souls we don't know what the Maker knows.

Nevertheless I marveled that I had not foreseen his suicide. I thought of myself when I was younger, and how many times I'd been tempted to take my own life. There were months, even years, when I was obsessed with the possibility of suicide, times even when I'd planned my own death down to the disposal of my remains. Indeed, every time I'd completed an assassination for The Right Man, skillfully dispatching another soul into the unknown, I'd been so tempted to take my own life that it was a marvel I'd survived. What would my life have amounted to, had I taken that step? I was almost weeping with gratitude suddenly that I'd been given the opportunity to do something, anything, that might be good. Anything, I whispered to myself as I walked along, anything at all that might be good. Vitale and Niccolò were alive and well. And the soul of Giovanni had apparently found rest. If I'd played the smallest part in any of it, I was too grateful for words. So why was I weeping? Why was I so sad? Why did I keep seeing Lodovico, dying with the poison in his mouth? No, this was no perfect victory, far from it.

And then there was Ankanoc, the real dybbuk of this adventure, and his words still echoing in my mind. When and how would I have to deal with Ankanoc from now on? Of course it had been foolish for me to think that I might see angels and not demons, that the one would not presuppose the other, and that some sinister personage would not manage to be more than a negative voice in my head. Yet I hadn't expected it. No, I hadn't. And still didn't know what to make of it. Fact was, I believed in God and always had, but I don't know if I have ever really believed in the Devil.

I couldn't get Ankanoc's face out of my mind, that bittersweet, charming expression. Surely before his fall, he had been an angel as beautiful as Malchiah, or so it seemed. Shocking to think of it, the vast airy firmament with its angels and demons, the world to which I belonged now more surely than any world I'd ever known.

I was growing tired. Why hadn't Malchiah taken me away? Perhaps because I had my heart set upon one more small experience here, and that was to find a cheery tavern, filled with laughter and light, where there was no lutenist playing at the moment.

At last I came to just such a bright and cheerful place with its door wide open to the night. A fire blazed in a crude cavern of a fireplace, and the rude tables and benches were thronged with men young and old, rich and poor, many with shining oily faces, some with heads bowed, dozing in the shadows, and indeed there were children there asleep on the laps of their fathers, or on bundles of rags on the dusty floor.

When I appeared with my lute, a lusty cry rose from the crowd. Cups were raised in greeting. I bowed, and I made my way towards a corner table where at once two tankards of ale were set down before me.

"Play, play, play," came the cries from all sides.

I closed my eyes and took a deep breath. How sweet the wine smelled, how delicious the malt. And how warm was the air, filled with the sounds of talk and laughter. I opened my eyes. Far on the other side of the tavern sat Ankanoc, looking exactly as he had at the Cardinal's banquet, peering at me, his eyes filled with tears.

I shook my head as if to say no to all he meant to offer, and now to answer him the best way I knew how—with song.

I began to strum and then to play, and within a moment had the place singing with me, though what the song was and how they knew it I could not guess. All the melodies I'd ever heard from this time I could easily now run through and it seemed to me I was happier here in these moments, surrounded by these crude and bold singers, than ever I'd been in all my strange life in this time, and maybe in any other. Ah, what broken creatures we are, and how we endure.

Indeed, deep dark memories came back to me, not of this world, but of the world I'd long ago left as a boy, when I'd stood on the street corner and strummed these old Renaissance songs for the bills people threw at my feet. I felt so sad for that boy, sad for his bitterness, sad for the mistakes he was going to make. I felt sad that he had lived so long with a locked heart and a ruptured conscience, sharpening the bitterness of his life on every cherished memory of pain that he carried in him day in and day out. And then I felt wonder that the seeds of goodness had lain dormant so long in him, waiting for the breath from an angel's lips.

Ankanoc was gone, though where or how I didn't know. All around me were convivial faces. People brought down their cups and tankards in time with my playing. I sang some of the old phrases I remembered, but mostly I played to their singing as melodies I'd never heard before came from the lute in my hands.

On and on I played until my soul was full of the warmth and the love around me, full of the light of the fire, and the light of so many faces, full with the sound of the strings of the lute, and the words becoming music, and then it seemed—right in the very middle of my boldest song, my sweetest, boldest most thumping and melodic song, I felt the air change, and the light brighten and I knew, I knew all these greasy shining faces that surrounded me were being transformed into something that was not corporeal at all, but rather notes of music, and it was a music of which I was only the barest part, and the music was rising higher and higher.

"Malchiah, I'm weeping," I whispered. "I don't want to leave them."

A long ribbon of laughter softly broke the darkness that surrounded me, and every syllable of it was picked up as if it were the kernel of a melody, full and entire, and destined now to mingle with another.

"Malchiah," I whispered.

And I felt his arms around me. I felt him cradling me as he lifted me. The music was made up of space as well as time and it seemed each note was a mouth from which another mouth sprang and then another and another.

He was cradling me as he carried me upward.

"Will I always love them so much? Will I always hate to leave them? Is that part of it, part of what I have to suffer?"

But the word "suffer" was the wrong word because it had all been too grand, too splendid, too golden. And I could hear his lips against my ear reminding me of that, and saying in the softest tones,

"You've done well, and now you know there are others waiting for you."

"This is the school of love," I said, "and every lesson is deeper, richer, finer."

I *saw* a vision of love; I *saw* that it was no one thing, but a great commingling of things both light and dark and fierce and tender, and my heart broke as the questions broke from my lips.

But no answer came except the anthems of Heaven.

CHAPTER THIRTEEN

SOMEONE WAS SHAKING ME. I WOKE UP, OUT OF A nightmare. Shmarya stood there in the darkness, his back to the pale light from the window. Nighttime streets below.

"You've been asleep for twenty-four hours," he said. We were in my room in the Mission Inn, and I lay on top of the rumpled comforter, my clothes twisted and moist, my body full of aching muscles. The room was cold.

The nightmare clung to me—full of all the telltale signs of dreams, the incoherent shifts, the distorted faces, the absurd and incomplete backdrops. It was utterly unlike the clarity of Angel Time.

I tried to hear again the angels singing, but there were only faint echoes, and a fragment of the nightmare rose, to blot them out.

Ankanoc had been arguing with me about the suicide of Lodovico. "According to your system," he had said over and over, "this poor soul goes into a blazing Hell. But there is no such place. His soul will reincarnate and he will have to learn what he failed to learn the first time." I'd seen the blazing Hell. I'd heard the screams of the damned. Ankanoc kept laughing. "You think I'm a devil? Why would I want to live in such a place?" Such a mocking smile, and then a wooden expression.

"You think you've been visited by angels of the Lord? Why would you be in such torment over so many things? If your personal God had forgiven you, if you had in fact turned to Him, wouldn't the Holy Spirit have flooded you with consolation and light? No, you know nothing of Heavenly Spirits. But don't let that frighten you. Welcome to the Human Race."

I sat up, bowed my head and prayed. "Lord, deliver me from this." I was dizzy and terribly thirsty. The sense of having failed, of having let Lodovico slip away into death, was as strong with me as it had been in Rome. And I was angry, angry that Ankanoc had come into my world, into my dreams, into my thoughts.

If your personal God had forgiven you, if you had in fact turned to Him, wouldn't the Holy Spirit have flooded you with consolation and light?

"It's finished now," said Shmarya. He had a quiet easy voice, resonant, but youthful, and he was dressed as I was dressed, in a blue cotton shirt and khaki pants.

He helped me off the bed. I went to the window and looked at my watch. It was 2:00 a.m. The streetlamps below gave the only illumination.

Memories of my time in Rome were crowding in, pervading the fragments of nightmare. "Let this dream go away, please!" I whispered.

To my surprise I felt Shmarya's hand on my shoulder. We were eye to eye. *I failed Lodovico. That one got away.*

"Stop struggling," he said. His expression was innocent, probing, his eyebrows knitting for an instant as he made his point. "This man's soul is not in your hands."

"The Maker *has* to know all things," I said. My voice broke. I could hear Ankanoc laughing, but this was memory. Shmarya was here. "And the Maker is the only one who can judge."

He nodded.

"Where's The Boss?" I asked. I meant Malchiah.

"He'll come soon enough," said Shmarya. "You need to take care of yourself now."

"Why do I have the feeling that you don't like him?"

"I love him," he said simply. "You know this. But he and I don't always agree. After all, I'm your guardian angel. My assignment is simple. You are my charge."

"And Malchiah?"

"Again, you know the answer to your own question. He's a Seraph. He's sent to answer the prayers of many. He knows things I can't know. He does things I'm not sent to do."

"But I thought you all know everything," I said. It sounded immediately stupid.

He shook his head.

"Then you can't tell me, can you, whether or not Lodovico went to Hell?" I insisted.

He shook his head.

I nodded. I pulled the blinds over the window. And I turned on the lamp by the bed.

It was powerfully comforting to see him so fully realized in the light. He looked as solid as anything else in the room. I wanted to touch him but I didn't, and then I remembered that he had just touched me.

I couldn't read anything into his blue eyes, or the relaxed way in which he studied me. He gave a little lift to his eyebrows, and then he said in a whisper, "Trust the Maker. What you think or what I think does not put a man in Hell."

"You know why I'm angry?"

He nodded.

I went on, "Because before I saw that man take his own life, I didn't believe in Hell. I didn't believe in the Devil or demons, and when I came to God, it was not out of fear of Hell."

He nodded.

"And now there is Ankanoc, and there is Hell."

He pondered this and then he shrugged.

"You've heard the voices of evil in the past," he said. "You've always known what evil is. You never lied to yourself."

"I have but I thought the voices came from within me. I thought all the evil I'd ever witnessed came from within individuals, that devils and Hell were old constructs. I felt myself become evil when I first took a human life. I felt myself grow ever more evil as I killed others. I can live with an evil that was inside myself, perhaps because I was able to repent. But now there's Ankanoc, a dybbuk, and I don't want to believe in such things."

"Does it really change things so much?"

"Shouldn't it?"

"How do we measure evil? By what evil does, isn't that so?" he waited. Then: "Nothing's changed. You've cast off the ways of Lucky the Fox, that's what matters. You're a Child of the Angels. A philosophy of evil does not alter those things."

I nodded. But I didn't find this perfectly comforting, true as it was. A wave of dizziness came over me. And the thirst was burning.

I went to the refrigerator in the little dining area, found a bottle of icy cold soda and drank it down in several gulps. The sheer sensuous pleasure of this quieted me and made me feel a little ashamed. Abstract thoughts yield so easily to bodily comfort, I thought.

"Don't you sometimes hate us?" I asked him.

"Never, and again you know that I don't."

"Are you trying to persuade me to ask genuine questions, instead of rhetorical questions?"

He laughed. It was a small agreeable laugh.

The caffeine in the soda was going to my head.

I went to the other windows one by one and drew the drapes, turning on the lamps that I passed—on the desk, and by the bed. The room felt a little safer now, for no good reason. Then I turned on the heat.

"You won't leave me, will you?" I asked.

"I never leave you," he said. His arms were folded. He was leaning against the wall by the window, looking at me across the room. Though his hair was red, his eyebrows were more golden, yet dark enough to give his expression a definite character. He was wearing shoes like mine, but not a wristwatch.

"I mean you won't go invisible!" I said with a little gesture of both hands. "You'll stay here till I've had a shower and changed clothes."

"You have things to do," he said. "If I'm distracting you, I should go."

"I can't call Liona at this hour," I said. "She's asleep."

"But what did you do last time when you came back?"

"Research, writing," I said. "I wrote down everything that had happened. I looked up more of the history of what I'd glimpsed. But you know The Boss is never going to let me show my writing about all this to anyone. That little dream of writing it down, being an author, putting it in books, it's gone."

I thought again of how I'd boasted to my former boss, The Right Man, that I would write about this great "something" that had happened to me, and about how I'd turned my life around. I'd told him to keep his eye on the bookstores, that someday he might find my name on the cover of a book. How foolish and impetuous that now seemed. I also recalled that I'd told him my real name, and I wished I had not done that. Why did I have to tell him that his trusted assassin, Lucky the Fox, was really Toby O'Dare?

Images of Liona and Toby flashed through my mind.

Those awful words of Ankanoc came back to me. *Wouldn't the Holy Spirit have flooded you with consolation and light?*

Well, I'd been filled with consolation and light when I'd spoken those words to The Right Man, and now I was confused. I didn't mind so much never telling anyone what I did for Malchiah. A Child of the Angels should keep confidential what he does if that is what is expected of him, just as secrecy had always been expected when I was assassin for The Right Man. How could I give the angels less than I'd given The Right Man? But there was more to it, this restlessness and confusion I felt. I felt fear. I was in the presence of a visible angel and I felt fear. It wasn't overwhelming, but it hurt, as if someone were subjecting me to an electrical current just strong enough to burn.

I took out another bottle of soda, savoring the coldness of it, even though I was still cold, and then drank again.

I sat down in the chair by the desk. "All right, you don't hate us, of course not," I said. "But you surely must become impatient with us, with our constant striving for a simple solution."

He smiled as if he liked the way I'd worded that, and then he answered,

"What would be the point of my becoming impatient?" he asked gently. "In fact, what is the point of your addressing my thoughts and emotions at all?" Again he shrugged.

"I don't understand when and how you intervene and when and how you don't."

"Ah, now that is a valid question. And I can give you a rule," he responded calmly. His voice was as gentle in all ways as Malchiah's voice, but he sounded younger, almost boyish. It was like a boy speaking with the restraint of an older man. "Your own free will is what matters," he explained, "and we will never interfere with that. So what we say or do, or how we appear, will always be governed by that imperative, that you have the free will to act."

I nodded. I finished off the second soda. My body felt like a sponge. "All right," I said, "but Malchiah showed me my whole life."

"He showed you your past," he said. "What's bothering you now is the future. You're talking to me but you are thinking of a multitude of things, all having to do with the future. You're wondering when and how you might see Liona again, and what will happen when you do. You're thinking of things you have to do in this world to erase the evidence of your hateful past as Lucky the Fox. You don't want your past deeds ever to harm Liona and Toby. And you're wondering why this last assignment from Malchiah was so different from your first assignment, and what the next assignment might involve."

All that was perfectly true. My mind was feverish with these questions.

"Where do I start?" I asked.

But I knew.

I went into the bathroom, and took the longest shower in my own personal history. And it did seem my own personal history consumed my thoughts. Liona and Toby. What did their presence in my life require me to do next? I didn't think about phone calls or checks to them, or visits. I mean, what did it require of me with regard to my ugly past? What did Lucky the Fox have to do about that past?

I shaved and dressed in a clean blue shirt and pressed jeans. I had a little mischievous desire to see if my guardian angel would change his garb because I'd changed mine.

Well, he didn't. He was sitting in the high-backed chair by the fireplace when I came out, and staring at the empty hearth.

"You're right," I said to him as if we'd never stopped talking. "I want to know all the answers as to the future, and as to my future. I have to remember that you are not here to make this easier for me."

"Well, in a way we are and in a way we aren't," he said. "But you have things to do now and you should do them. Do again what profited you the most before."

He had a slight dip to his eyebrows, his pupils moving ever so slightly but constantly, as though in watching me, he was watching some immense display of movement and detail that I couldn't comprehend.

"You spend too much time studying our faces," he offered. "You'll never be able to read us in this way. We couldn't explain to you the way we think even if we wanted to."

"Can your facial expression be dishonest, or deceiving?" I asked.

"No," he said, with a placid smile.

"Do you enjoy being visible to me?"

"Yes," he said. "We enjoy the physical universe. We always have. We enjoy your physicality. We find it interesting."

I was fascinated.

"Do you enjoy talking to me so that I can actually hear your voice?" I asked. "Do you really like it?"

"Yes," he said. "I like it very much."

"You must have had a horrible ten years when I was a killer," I said.

He laughed without making a sound, his eyes moving over the ceiling. Then he looked at me. "Not my best time," he said. "I have to admit."

I nodded, as if I'd caught him in a startling series of admissions, but of course I had caught him in nothing.

I went into the little kitchen area and made a pot of coffee. Finally when I had the first cup the way I wanted it, I turned back to him, sipping the coffee, savoring the heat the way I'd savored the coldness of the soda before.

"Why was Ankanoc allowed to test me?" I asked. "Why was he allowed to lead me off like that in Rome?"

"You're asking *me*?" he answered. Again came that small shrug. "Special angels come for those who have a special destiny. And special demons target those same individuals in special ways."

"So there's more to come." I said. "He'll never give up."

He pondered this and indicated he couldn't answer. Just a little gesture with his hands, and a little lift to his eyebrows.

"What did you learn about him?" he asked.

"He chose the way of reason to attack me, old arguments, theories I'd read. He ventured into New Age philosophy, the testimony of those who've traveled out of body, claimed to have had near-death experiences. But he made a hash of it. The point is, he attacked my faith, through reason, rather than my shaky self-control."

He drifted into thought again, or into something like it. He looked to be about my age, I figured, but why he'd chosen to appear with red hair I couldn't guess, and it seemed his body was a little thicker all over than Malchiah's body. These things had to mean something but what? There might be rules to all this, a vast system of them, but it might be far too intricate and involved for me to understand.

He spoke up suddenly, bringing me back to the conversation.

"There's an old story," he said, "about a saint who once said, 'Even when the Prince of Darkness takes the form of an angel of light, you'll know him by his reptilian tail.' "

I laughed. "I've heard that story," I said. "I knew the saint once. Well, Ankanoc didn't have a reptilian tail."

"But he gave himself away, nevertheless. You pegged him for what he was early on—by his speech, the unkind remarks he made about human beings."

"That's exactly right," I said. "And also by the way in which he used the New Age viewpoints on questions of life and death and why we're here. What's fascinating about those viewpoints is that they're put forth by a whole variety of thinkers, that certain patterns of thought emerge from psychic pioneers all over the globe. But Ankanoc treated them as if they were dogma and he tried to ram that dogma home."

"Keep this in mind," he said. "No matter what he does and says, he will always give himself away. Demons are too full of hate and rage to be too clever. Don't overestimate them. That might be as bad as underestimating them. And if you call him by name, he must answer you, so he's not likely to try a disguise again."

"So you're saying that demons aren't as smart as angels."

"Perhaps they could be," he said, "but their state of mind interferes with their intelligence. It interferes with their observations, and their conclusions. It interferes with everything that they do. Theirs is a hideous predicament. They refuse to admit that they have lost."

That was beautiful. I liked it. I liked the puzzle of it and the truth of it.

"Do you know him personally?" I asked.

"Personally?" He burst out laughing. "Personally!" he said again with a gleaming smile. "Toby, you are a fascinating young man. No, I don't know him personally. I don't think he would give me the time of day." He laughed again. "He doesn't think he has to worry about me, a 'mere guardian angel.' It's Malchiah who drives him to the brink. He has a great deal to learn."

"So after work, when I'm asleep for instance, you and Ankanoc couldn't go to a café together in Angel Time for a drink."

"No," he said, laughing again. "And I'm not off work when you're sleeping, by the way. You probably know that very well."

"Were you there, with me in Rome?" I asked.

"Yes, of course. I'm always with you. I'm your guardian angel, I told you. I've been with you since before you were born."

"But in Rome, you couldn't come to me, appear to me, help me?" I asked.

"What do you think?" he asked.

"Oh, not again. You angels keep turning the questions around."

"Don't we, though!" he whispered. "But now we both know one reason, at least, why you're so troubled. You're angry that I didn't come to you and help you. But Malchiah came, did he not?"

"Finally, yes," I responded. "He came when it was all over. But couldn't either of you have given me a hint that this creature was waylaying me with extraordinary means?"

He shrugged.

"I think you must bow to Malchiah's wishes," I said.

"That is one way of describing things," he said. "Malchiah is a Seraph. I am not."

"Why are you here now?" I asked.

"Because you need me and you want me to be here, and you're restless and your ideas of what to do next are unformed. That's part of it, at least. But I think it's time you started doing what you did after your last assignment. So perhaps I should go."

"I wish you were always visible."

"You think that's what you wish. You have a short memory. I am not here to interfere with your being a man."

"Do Children of Angels get lonely?" I asked.

"You're lonely, aren't you?" he asked. "Do you think any amount of angelic company can take away human desire? We're here because you're human. You'll be a human being till the day you die."

"I wish I knew what you really looked like—!" I said.

The atmosphere around me instantly changed. It was as if some force had shaken the entire room, perhaps the entire building, and certainly my entire point of view.

The contents of the room faded. Gravity was gone. I wasn't standing anywhere. An immense sound filled my ears, a sound vaguely akin to the reverberations of a huge gong, and at the same time an unending white light filled my vision, shot through with great arcing splashes of gold. All I could see was this exploding light. There was a core to it, a pulsing, vibrant core, from which the enormous sweeps of gold emanated, and quite suddenly it was beyond all the language I had. I struggled in my brain for concepts to describe it, to seize it and hold on to it, but this was not possible. There was movement, tremendous movement, something like convolutions or eruptions. But the words mean nothing compared to what I saw. I had a momentous sense of *recognition.* I heard myself gasp aloud, "Yes," but this was over before it had begun. The light defined a space too vast for me to see or grasp, and yet I saw it, saw its limitless reaches. The sound had reached a searing pitch. The light contracted and was gone.

I lay on the floor, staring at the domed ceiling above me. I closed my eyes. What I could reproduce in my mind was nothing, nothing compared to what I'd just seen and heard.

"Forgive me," I whispered. "I should have known."

CHAPTER FOURTEEN

I WENT TO THE COMPUTER FIRST AND FOREMOST FOR the information I wanted about my time in Rome.

I wasn't surprised that I could not find the names of those I'd visited in any historical record.

But the horrid and cruel incident that had befallen Giovanni's son in Florence was recorded in more than one place. No names were given, of the man accused of blaspheming the images, or of his surviving family. But it was definitely the same incident and I was left with a strong memory of the elderly Giovanni, staring at me in the synagogue, after I'd stopped playing the lute.

I had no doubt that my mission had been amongst real people. And I read on amongst the various sources about the times.

I soon learned what I should never have forgotten, that Rome was sacked in 1527, at which time thousands of lives were lost. Some sources said the whole Jewish community was annihilated at this time.

This meant just about everyone I'd known in Rome might have died at this point in history, only some nine years or less after the time of my visitation.

I thanked God that I hadn't known this part of the story while I was there. But more importantly, I realized in an instant what I hadn't grasped in my entire selfish life: that it is imperative for us in this world not to know for certain what the future holds. There could be no present if the future were known.

I might have known this intellectually at the age of twelve. But now it struck me with a mystical force. And it reminded me that I was dealing with creatures in Malchiah and Shmarya who knew much more about the future than I wanted to know. To be angry with them or resentful of them because they lived with this burden made no sense.

There were many things I wanted to ponder.

Instead I typed a brief and concise account of all that had happened to me since my last "report." I wrote down not only the story of my adventure in Rome, but also the story of my meeting with Liona and Toby, and what had taken place.

It occurred to me as I finished that there were distinct reasons why my second assignment had been different from my first. In the first adventure, I'd been sent to do something fairly straightforward—save a family and a community from an unjust charge. I'd solved the problem presented to me with duplicity, but there had not been the slightest doubt in my mind that it was the right path to take.

Maybe angels couldn't encourage lies as I had done in Angel Time, but they had let me do it, and I felt that I knew why.

Many in this world have lied to save themselves from evil and injustice. Who would not have lied to save Jews in our own time from genocide at the hands of the Third Reich?

But my second assignment had involved no such situation. I had sought to use the truth to solve the problems confronting me, and found it a very complex and hard thing to do indeed.

So was it safe to assume each of my missions would be more complex than the last? I was just beginning to reflect on these things, when finally I broke off.

It was noon. I'd been awake for ten hours, and writing for

most of that. I'd eaten nothing. I might start seeing angels who weren't there.

I put on my jacket and went down for lunch in the Mission Inn Restaurant, and found myself sitting there pondering again after the dishes had been cleared away.

I was drinking my last cup of coffee when I noticed a young man at another table staring at me, though when I fixed on him, he pretended to be reading his paper.

I let myself stare at him for a good while. He seemed neither angel nor dybbuk. Just a man. He was younger than me, and as I watched him, he looked at me more than once, and finally got up from the table and left.

I wasn't surprised to see him in the lobby, seated in one of the large chairs, with his eyes turned towards the restaurant entrance.

I memorized what I saw: he was young, maybe four or five years my junior. He had short brown wavy hair and almost pretty blue eyes. He'd worn dark-rimmed glasses when he'd been reading. And he was dressed a bit nattily in a well-fitted brown corduroy Norfolk jacket, with a white turtleneck sweater, and gray pants. There had been a certain vulnerability to his expression, an eagerness, that completely negated any question in my mind of danger, but I didn't like it that I was being noticed by anybody, and I wondered who he was and why he'd been there.

If he was another angel on the case, I wanted to know. And if he was another devil, well, he didn't have the presence or the confidence of Ankanoc and I couldn't figure his approach.

The question of danger was a real one. Lucky the Fox had always had his antennae out for those who might be watching him, whether sent by his enemies or his boss.

But this man simply did not look the part of a dangerous individual at all. No cop, or agent of The Right Man, would have stared so obviously at me. Another assassin would have never made himself known. If anything the incident served to make me aware of how very safe I felt, though I still had some lingering anxiety about having told my real name to The Right Man.

I forgot about it, found a quiet place on a patio outside, where the sun was pleasantly warm and the breeze cool, and I called Liona.

The sound of her voice almost brought tears to my eyes. And only as we chatted did I realize it had been five days since she and Toby had flown home.

"Believe me," I said, "I wanted to call you before now. I've been thinking about you both since you left. I want to see you again and soon."

She wanted that too, she said. All I had to do was name the time and place. She explained she'd been to her lawyer with all the legal documents I'd given her. Her father was pleased that I'd taken responsibility for my son in this way.

"But Toby, there's something that's been bothering me," she explained. "Do your cousins down here know you're alive?"

"No, they don't," I admitted. "And if I come back there, well, I feel I have to see them."

"There's something I didn't tell you before, but I think you should know. About three years ago, when you were declared . . ."

"Legally dead?" I offered.

"Yes, well, your cousin Matt took all your old things out of storage, and he came by and gave us some of your old books. Toby, he knew, at least I had told him that Toby was your son."

"That's good, Liona, I'm glad. I don't mind at all about Matt knowing. I can't blame you for telling him."

"Well, there's more to it than that. You know my father, you know he's a doctor first and foremost."

"Yes?"

"He asked Matt for permission to run some DNA tests on the evidence taken from your mom's apartment. Dad said he wanted it for medical reasons, to know if there were any medical problems in the family that Toby might . . ."

"I understand." I went cold all over. I struggled to keep my voice steady. "That's fine. That's completely reasonable," I lied. "Matt said yes, and your father tested my family's DNA and Little Toby's DNA." *Which means there is a record of DNA close to that of Lucky the Fox in a file.* My heart was skipping a beat or two. "You're not trying to tell me there was some congenital problem—."

"No. I just wanted you to know. We thought you were dead, Toby."

"Liona, don't worry. It's all fine. And I'm glad you did it. Your father knows for sure that Little Toby is mine."

"Well, that was part of it, too," she confessed. "He has proof of affinity, as they call it, and that will have to do."

"Listen, my love," I said. "I have some work to do. I have to talk to my employer. And when I find out what my schedule is, I'll call you right away. Now I'm on a prepaid cell here and you have this number. Call me whenever you want."

"Oh, I won't bother you, Toby," she insisted.

"If I don't pick up, it means I can't," I said.

"Toby?"

"Yes."

"I want you to know something, but I don't want it to frighten you."

"Of course. What?"

"I love you," she said.

I let out a long sigh. "Am I ever glad to hear that," I whispered. "Because my heart is in your hands."

I clicked off.

I was acutely happy and acutely distressed. She loved me.

And I loved her, and then all the other dark truths intruded, faster than I could name them or recognize them. No one tracking Lucky the Fox had ever obtained a sample of DNA, but now Lucky the Fox and Toby O'Dare were known to be one and the same to The Right Man, and there was DNA of Toby O'Dare's family in a file in New Orleans. And I had foolishly told The Right Man that I had come from New Orleans.

"There are things you have to do," Shmarya had said in so many words, and he had been right. I couldn't do anything about this DNA question, and indeed, it might not matter, considering how my various hits had been accomplished, but there were other things I could do and ought to do promptly.

I checked out of the inn and drove to Los Angeles.

My apartment was as I'd left it, with the doors wide open to the patio, and the jacaranda blossoms still littered the quiet street below.

I dressed in some old clothes, and drove to the garage where I'd kept my trucks and my disguises and my other materials for some two or three years. For two hours, carefully gloved and gowned, I destroyed things.

Now, I had never brewed my poisonous concoctions from so-called "controlled substances." Just about every lethal cocktail I'd ever devised had been from over-the-counter drugs or flowers and herbs available everywhere. I'd used micro-syringes any diabetic can buy without difficulty. Nevertheless the assemblage of items in the garage constituted a kind of evidence and I felt much better when every last bottle had been emptied and every last package burned. Ashes went down the drains. And a great deal of water went after them.

I wiped down the trucks very carefully, and then drove them to different areas of downtown Los Angeles where I left them with the keys in the ignition. The licenses and registration were a dead end, so I had no fears there. I walked for about six blocks after leaving the last truck, speculating that all of them might have already been stolen, and I took a cab back to the vicinity of the garage.

The place was now empty. I left the doors opened and unlocked.

Within a matter of hours homeless people would come into this place, seeking shelter or whatever valuables they might find. Their personal belongings, their fingerprints and their DNA would soon be everywhere, and that was a fitting end, as it had been in the past, for any such garage that Lucky the Fox had used.

I drove home feeling a little more safe, and feeling that Liona and Toby were a little more safe. I couldn't be sure of anything, really. But I was doing what I could to protect Lucky the Fox from harming them.

The anxiety I felt was considerable and inevitable. I realized that no matter what happened with me and Malchiah and Shmarya, I was becoming Toby O'Dare in the world, and Toby O'Dare had never really existed before as he did now. I felt naked and vulnerable, and I didn't like it. In fact, I was surprised how much I didn't like it.

That night I took a plane to New York.

And the next day, I did the same things in the garage that I kept there. It had been almost a year since I'd been in that particular way station, and I didn't like going back there at all. New York had too many shocking memories for me, and I felt especially sensitive to them now. But I knew this had to be done. I dumped the vehicles in areas where they would most certainly be stolen, and left the garage finally as I had done the other one, open to whoever might wander in.

I wanted to leave New York then, but there was something else I wanted badly to do. I had to think about it a great deal before executing my little plan. I spent the evening and the next morning doing just that. I was very glad that the angels weren't visibly with me. I understood now why they were not. And the terms of my new existence were making a little more sense to me.

When afternoon came, I left my hotel and went out walking to find a Catholic church.

I must have walked for hours before coming upon a church that looked and felt the way that I wanted it to feel; and this was all purely feelings, as I had no thoughts on the matter at all.

I knew only that I was somewhere in Midtown when I rang the bell at the rectory and told the woman who answered that I wanted to go to confession. She stared at my hands. It was warm and I was wearing gloves.

"Can you ask the oldest priest in the house?" I asked her.

I wasn't sure she heard or understood. She showed me into a small sparsely furnished parlor with a table and several upright wooden chairs. There was a small window with dusty curtains revealing part of a yard paved in asphalt. A large old-fashioned crucifix hung on the wall. I sat very still, and I prayed.

It seemed I waited half an hour before a very elderly priest came in. Had it been a young priest, I would probably have left a donation and gone out without a word. As it was, this man was ancient, somewhat shrunken, with an extremely large squarish head, and with wire-rimmed glasses that he took off and set on the table to his right.

He took out his requisite purple stole, a long thin strip of silk required for the hearing of confessions, and he put it around his neck. His gray hair was thick and messy. He sat back in his wooden chair and closed his eyes.

"Bless me, Father, for I have sinned," I said. "It has been over ten years since my last confession and I have been too far from the Lord. For ten years I've committed terrible sins more numerous than I can mention, and I can only estimate how many times I have done any one bad thing."

There was no change in his demeanor whatsoever.

"I took life willfully and deliberately," I said. "I told myself I was killing men who were bad, but in fact I destroyed the lives of innocent persons, especially in the beginning, and I cannot now name how many there were. After those first and most terrible crimes, I went to work for an agency which used me to kill others, and I obeyed their orders without question, annihilating about three persons on average a year for ten years. This agency told me we were The Good Guys. And I think you understand why I can tell you no more about this than what I've said so far. I cannot tell you who these people were, nor for whom specifically I did these things. I can only tell you that I am sorry for them, and I have vowed on my knees never to take life again. I have repented with my whole heart. I have also resolved to walk a path of reparation, to make up in my remaining years for what I did in these last ten. I have a spiritual director who knows the full extent of what I have done and is directing me to reparation. I am confident God has forgiven me but I have come for absolution to you."

"Why?" he asked. He had a deep sonorous baritone voice. He did not move or open his eyes.

"Because I want to go back to Communion," I said. "I want to be in my church with others who believe in God as I do, and I want to go to the banquet table of the Lord once again."

He remained as before.

"This spiritual director?" he asked. "Why doesn't he give you absolution?" He said the last word with force, his deep voice almost a rumble in his chest.

"He's not a Roman Catholic priest," I said. "He's a person of impeccable credentials and judgment, and his advice has guided my repentance. But I'm a Catholic man, and that's why I've come to you." I went on to explain that I'd committed other sins, sins of lust and sins of greed and sins of pedestrian unkindness. I listed everything that I could think of. Of course I had missed Mass on Sundays. I had missed Holy Days of Obligation. I had not kept feast days such as Christmas or Easter. I had lived away from God. I went on and on. I told him that as the result of my early indiscretions, I had a child, and I had now made contact with that child, and that almost all the money I had earned from my past actions was being set aside for the child and the mother of the child. I would keep what I required to sustain me, but I would never kill again.

"I beg you to give me absolution," I said, finally.

A silence fell between us. "You realize some innocent person might be charged with the crimes you've committed?" he ventured. His baritone voice quavered slightly.

"It's never happened to my knowledge. Well, except for my blundering actions in the beginning, everything I did for hire was covert. But even in the case of those early murders, to my knowledge, no one was ever charged. And I did have some knowledge, and no, no one was ever charged."

"If someone is charged you have to come forward," he said. He sighed but he didn't open his eyes.

"I will."

"And you will not kill again even for these people who call themselves The Good Guys," he murmured.

"Correct. Never. No matter what happens I will not."

He sat quiet for a moment. "This spiritual director," he started.

"I ask that you not press me on his identity, any more than you would press me on the identity of those for whom I did the killing. I ask that you trust me that I am telling you the truth. I've come here for no other reason."

He reflected. The deep voice rolled out of him once more. "You know that to lie in the confessional is sacrilege."

"I have left out nothing. I have lied about nothing. And I thank you for your compassion in not pressing me for further details."

He didn't respond. One gnarly wrinkled hand came down uneasily on the surface of the table.

"Father," I said, "it's hard for a man like me to be a responsible person in the world. It's impossible for me to confide my history to anyone. It's impossible for me ever to bridge the gap between me and those innocent human beings who have never done the awful things that I have done. I am consecrated now to God. I will work for Him and for Him only. But I am a man in this world, and I want to go to my church in this world with other men and women, and I want to hear Mass with them, and I want to reach out and hold their hands as we say the Lord's Prayer together under God's roof. I want to approach Holy Communion with them and receive it with them. I want to be part of my church in this world in which I live."

He took a deep rattling breath.

"Say your Act of Contrition," he said.

Sudden panic. This was the only part of this I hadn't gone over in detail in my mind. I couldn't remember the whole prayer.

I put everything out of my thoughts except that I was talking to the Maker.

" 'O my God, I am heartily sorry for having offended Thee, and I despise all my sins because they have separated me from Thee, and though I fear the loss of Heaven and the pains of Hell, I am sorry for my sins because of that separation, and because of the terrible harm I have done to the souls whose journeys I have interrupted, and I know that I can never undo those wrongs done them no matter what I do. Please, Dear

God, affirm my repentance and give me the grace to live it day in and day out. Let me be your child. Let my remaining years be years of serving you.' "

Without ever opening his eyes, he raised his hand and gave me the absolution.

"Penance, Father?" I asked.

"Do what this spiritual director tells you," he said.

He opened his eyes, took off the stole, folded it and put it back in his pocket. He was about to leave without ever once looking at me.

I took an envelope out of my pocket. It was stuffed with big bills, all of which had been wiped completely clean of prints. I gave it to him.

"For you or for the church or whatever you want, my donation." I said.

"Not required, young man, you know that," he said. He glanced at me once with large watery eyes and then away.

"I know that, Father. I want to give you this donation."

He took the envelope and he left the room.

I walked outside, felt the spring air warm around me and caressing and soothing, and then I started to walk back towards my hotel. The light was sweet and gentle, and I felt an overwhelming love for the many random people I passed. Even the cacophony of the city comforted me, the roar and clatter of the traffic like the breath of a being, or the beat of a heart.

When I came to St. Patrick's Cathedral, I went in and sat down in a pew and waited until the evening Mass.

This vast beautiful space was as comforting to me as it had ever been. I'd come here often both before and after I'd begun my life for The Right Man. I'd often stared at the distant high altar for hours, or walked up and down the side aisles of the church inspecting the magnificent art, and the various shrines. This for me was the quintessential Catholic church, with its soaring arches and its unapologetic grandeur. I was painfully glad that I was here now, painfully glad of all that had recently happened to me.

A good crowd gathered just as it was getting dusk outside. I went up closer to the altar. I wanted to hear the Mass and to see it. At the moment of the Consecration of the bread and wine, I bowed my head and I wept. I didn't care who noticed this. Didn't matter. When we stood to say the Lord's Prayer, I took off my gloves and reached out to those on either side of me as we said the words.

When I went to Communion, I could not disguise the tears. But it didn't matter. If anybody noticed, I did not notice that person. I was as alone as I'd ever been, comfortable in my anonymity and in this ritual. And yet I was connected with all here, I was part of this place and this moment, and this felt very simply glorious.

And you can perfectly well cry when you go to Communion in a Catholic church.

There was a moment afterwards when I knelt in the pew with my head bowed, thinking about how the world, the great real world about me, might view what I was doing here. The modern world so detests rituals.

What did rituals mean to me? Everything, because they were the patterns that reflected my deepest feelings and commitments.

I had been visited by angels. I had followed their loving advice. But that was one miracle. And this, the Miracle of the True Presence of Our Blessed Lord in the bread and the wine, was another. And this miracle is what mattered to me now.

I didn't care what the great world thought. I didn't care about points of theology or logic. Yes, God is everywhere, yes, God pervades everything in the universe, and God is also here. God is here now in this way, within me. This ritual has brought me to God and God to me. I let my understanding of this pass out of words and into a silent acceptance.

"God, please protect Liona and Toby from Lucky the Fox and all that he has done, please. Let me live to serve Malchiah; let me live for Liona and my son."

I said many other prayers—I prayed for my family; I prayed for each and every soul whom I had ushered into eternity; I prayed for Lodovico; I prayed for The Right Man; I prayed for the nameless and the innumerable whose lives had been disrupted by the evils I had done. And then I gave way to the Prayer of Quiet, only listening for the voice of God.

Mass had been over for about half an hour. I left the pew, genuflecting as in the old days, and went down the aisle, feeling a marvelous sense of peace and pure happiness.

As I reached the back of the church, I saw that the side door on the left was open, but not the main doors, so I went that way towards the street.

There was a man standing just inside the door with his back to the light and something struck me about him, which caused me to glance at him directly.

It was the young man from the Mission Inn. He wore the same brown corduroy jacket, with a white shirt open at the neck under a sweater vest. He stared right at me. He looked emotional, as if he was about to speak. But he didn't.

My heart thudded in my ears. What the Hell was he doing here? I walked past him and outside and started down the street away from my hotel. I was trembling. I tried to run through all the possibilities that might explain this strange sighting but in truth there weren't very many. Either this was a coincidence or he was following me. And if he was following me then he might have seen me go to the garage in Los Angeles and the garage in New York! This was absolutely insupportable.

Never in all my years as Lucky the Fox had I ever been aware of anyone following me. Again, I cursed the day I'd told The Right Man my real name, but I couldn't fit this strangely vulnerable-looking young man into any scenario involving The Right Man. So who was he?

The longer I walked up Fifth Avenue, the more certain I was that this guy was right behind me. I could feel him. We were approaching Central Park. The traffic moving downtown was thick and noisy, the harsh sound of the car horns striking at my nerves, the exhaust fumes making my eyes water. Yet I was thankful we were here, in New York, amid the early evening crowds, with people on all sides of us.

But what the Hell was I going to do about this guy? What could I do? And it occurred to me with utter finality that I absolutely couldn't do what Lucky the Fox might have done. I couldn't do him violence. No matter what he knew that was no longer an option. I was suddenly maddened by that fact. I felt trapped by it.

I wanted to look back to see if I could spot him and as I stepped off the curb to cross the street I glanced uneasily over my shoulder.

Suddenly two firm hands grabbed me by the arms and pulled me sharply back. My ankle caught on the curb. I stumbled but I stumbled backwards. A taxicab roared past me and across Fifth, against the light, inciting shouts from all sides. The cab had almost run me down.

I was badly shaken.

Of course I thought it was Malchiah or Shmarya who had saved me from this. But when I turned to see who it was, there was the young man standing there, inches from me.

"That car could have killed you," he said. He backed up. His voice was an educated voice, in no way familiar to me.

The taxicab slammed into something or someone on the other side of Fifth. The noise was horrific.

People were going around us now and letting us know in no uncertain terms that we were blocking the sidewalk.

But I wanted a good look at this person, so I didn't move, and he stood just a few feet from me looking into my eyes in much the same way that he had in the cathedral.

He really was young, early twenties at most. He seemed somehow to be imploring me.

I turned and walked over to the nearest wall and stood there. He came with me. This was exactly what I expected. I was bristling with hostility. I was angry, angry that he'd followed me, angry that he'd saved me from the cab. I was angry he wasn't more afraid of me, that he dared come this close to me, that he had let himself be seen so fearlessly.

I was in a perfect fury.

"How long have you been following me?" I demanded. I was trying not to grit my teeth, I was so angry.

He didn't respond. He was badly shaken himself. I could see all the little signals in his face, the way his lips moved without forming words, the way his pupils danced as he looked at me.

"What do you want from me?" I demanded.

"Lucky the Fox," he said in a low intimate voice. "I want you to talk to me. I want you to tell me who sent you to kill my father."

The End
January 29, 2010

Author's Note

SONGS OF THE SERAPHIM ARE WORKS OF FICTION. However, real events and real persons inspire some of what takes place in these books. And every effort has been made to present the historical milieu of the novels with full accuracy.

The tragic maiming and subsequent mutilation of a Jewish boy in Florence in 1493 is described in detail in *Public Life in Renaissance Florence* by Richard G. Trexler, published by Cornell University Press. However, nothing is noted in any source that I found as to the identity of the young man, his relatives or his ultimate fate. I have used these sources to create a fictional version of the incident in this novel.

The flower called "the Purple Death" is fictional. For obvious reasons I did not want to include details regarding a real poison in this book.

My principal sources for this novel were two books by Cecil Roth, one very large work entitled *The History of the Jews of Italy* and a shorter but no less informative work, *The Jews of the Renaissance,* both published by the Jewish Publication Society of America. Also of tremendous help was part of Jewish Community Series and translated by Moses Hadas and also published by the Jewish Publication Society of America. I was also helped by *Jewish Life in Renaissance Italy* by Robert Bonfil, translated by Anthony Oldcorn and published by the University of Chicago Press. *The Renaissance Popes* by Gerard Noel was also helpful, and I am indebted to Noel for the fact that Pope Julius II dined on caviar every day at lunch.

I consulted many other books on Rome, on Italy, on the Jews throughout the world during this period of history, and these books are far too numerous to name here. Any student interested in further study will find abundant resources at his or her fingertips.

Once again, I want to acknowledge Wikipedia, the online encyclopedia.

With regard to the Renaissance lute, I listened to a good deal of music while writing this book, but was singularly inspired by a compact disc called *The Renaissance Lute* by Ronn McFarlane. Let me recommend to the listener selection No. 7, entitled only "Pessemeze." This piece of music proved particularly haunting, and I imagine my hero, Toby, playing it during his concluding hours in Renaissance Italy.

Once again let me acknowledge the existence and the beauty of the Mission Inn in Riverside, California, and the beautiful Mission of San Juan Capistrano.

And let me thank again with special fervor and gratitude the Jewish Publication Society of America for all they have done for research in the field of Jewish history.

A NOTE ON THE TYPE

THIS BOOK was set in Adobe Garamond. Designed for the Adobe Corporation by Robert Slimbach, the fonts are based on types first cut by Claude Garamond (c. 1480–1561). Garamond was a pupil of Geoffroy Tory and is believed to have followed the Venetian models, although he introduced a number of important differences, and it is to him that we owe the letter we now know as "old style." He gave to his letters a certain elegance and feeling of movement that won their creator an immediate reputation and the patronage of Francis I of France.

Composed by Creative Graphics,
Allentown, Pennsylvania
Printed and bound by Berryville Graphics,
Berryville, Virginia
Designed by Virginia Tan